Tangerine Sky

By

Karelyn Kline

Tangerine Sky

ISBN 978-1-7325036-0-1

Request for information should be addressed to:
Curry Brothers Marketing and Publishing Group
P.O. Box 247
Haymarket, VA 20168

Table of Contents

Dedication

Tangerine Sky is dedicated to all those who so willingly offered suggestions, support, and effort toward its conclusion.

Acknowledgments

Carol wishes first to express gratitude to her Heavenly Father whose periodic nudging and assurance of His guidance led her to the joys of writing.

Her chosen pen name offers tribute to her earthly father, Kline Wonch, for his wise and caring guidance throughout her growing up years. This includes the mother who stood by him in the huge responsibility of preparing a child for the demands of life.

She gratefully thanks her sister, Charlene Laper, for offering helpful suggestions and critiquing. A thank you also goes to her nephew, Collin Blatt, for his computer expertise. Deep appreciation is due to the many people of our Mexico villages whose lives, experiences, and faith are reflected in some of the book's episodes.

Much appreciation goes to Tanya Ringlever for her kind offer of typing. Great credit belongs to Gregory and Robin Hetherington for their helpful advice, and cover design. Without these numerous supporters, Tangerine Sky would not have come into existence.

And last but not least, a big thank you to Brittany Robati of Ann Brown Editing, as well much gratitude to Curry Brothers Publishing.

Chapter 1
Good Bye

Nancy tossed her covers aside as a warm light began to turn her bedroom wall to gold. She slipped from bed to stand at her east window. The sky was aglow with predawn color. "Oh, Jesus!" she whispered. "My tangerine sky! My parting gift! Not parting from you, Jesus—not ever! But from this dear place."

Her eyes scanned the yard, the buildings. "So many memories… And now separation from Mom, Daddy, and Joey." She paused, "and from Dan… How I've prayed that they all understand!"

Nancy had pled long and earnestly for God's will as she was contemplating this year of ministry across the border in a Mexico village. There she could use her nursing skills. She could tell children the beautiful stories of Jesus and His love for them. She would perhaps meet with women or teens to explore the wonders of God's Word. She could only imagine the possibilities.

At last, she was assured that this was God's plan. She'd been filled with such excitement and anticipation, but this morning with leave-taking only a few hours away, a small cloud of dread shadowed her eagerness.

"Jesus, please make it easier on my family, and on Dan." And still gazing at the gorgeous dawn, "Jesus, can you please give me a tangerine sky sometimes in Puesta del Sol? Surely, Lord, a village called 'Sunset' will have some of the same lovely skies that You give me here." It was a comforting thought.

She turned from the window, snatched up her robe and hurried downstairs to the kitchen. Mom was just taking a pan of scrambled eggs from the stove. Hot biscuits were on the table.

"Oh, Mom, I should have been here helping you," Nancy sighed.

"Not this morning, my dear. I wanted you to have all the rest you could for your big day ahead.

The men will be in soon," she added. Mom smiled as she thought of how her youngest always straightened his shoulders when she fondly addressed both husband and son as "the men."

Almost as soon as mother spoke, the two pushed through the kitchen door.

"Your things are all in the truck, Nancy," Dad announced with that special look he often gave her. Joey, of course, assumed the martyr complex.

"You sure you're going to need all that stuff? 'Bout broke my back lifting that mountain of suitcases."

Nancy punched his upper arm playfully. "With muscles like that, I don't think you suffered much." She pulled him to her and kissed the top of his head.

"I do thank you both," she added. "And Joey, I'll bring you back something very special from Mexico for your heroic efforts."

"How about one of those leather saddles with tooling for Champ?" he bantered.

"I think you're a horseman with some extravagant ideas, little brother," Nancy laughed.

Breakfast finished, they were soon settled in the front seat of the pickup.

"Good thing we're all Slim Jims," Dad grinned, as they all four wedged themselves together in one seat.

"Aw, there's still room for one of Nancy's fat suitcases between us," said Joey.

Everyone tried to keep the conversation light and cheerful as they headed south toward the border. Nearing their destination, Nancy wanted to interject her anticipation of the planned Christmas break.

"Know what I'm looking forward to? Just as soon as Christmas activities are over in Puesta del Sol, I'll be home for a few days. It won't be long. It's already September."

"By that time, you'll have forgotten all your English. You'll be talking to us in Spanish," said Joey.

"Then you'd better pay attention in that class you're taking so you and I can talk about all our Christmas secrets together." Nancy winked at Dad over Joey's head and clasp Mom's hand in hers.

"You'll call often won't you, Dear?" Mom asked.

"Of course I will. Probably every day," Nancy reassured her. "I'll be telling you all about my little house and the car the Mission has waiting for me to use. I hope the car is blue," she laughed. "But I'll really not complain whatever the hue."

"Wow! What a boss you have! A house! A car!" Joey exclaimed.

"Well, you know who my Boss really is. It's good to check out His plan carefully before you make a decision."

"I know," Joey admitted, serious for once.

Dan was to meet them at the border. They spied his well-seasoned Chevy as they swung into the customs area. He was quickly out of his car and headed in their direction. With a brisk, "Good morning" for all and a smile directed at Nancy, he bounded into the pickup bed beside the luggage.

At the crossing point, Nancy handed her luggage keys to the official. He opened a couple of the larger pieces, fingered through them and relocked each.

"Where you headed?" he asked as he returned the keys.

"Just to the bus station," Dad answered, "except for my daughter here, she needs papers to stay in the country longer."

"Right there!" The customs officer flicked a thumb toward the building to his right.

The family waited while Nancy filled out forms, presented her passport, and paid the required fees.

Then on to the bus station where Dad, Dan, and Joey unloaded luggage while Mom and Nancy walked to the ticket window. Finally, Nancy was able to put her Spanish to good use by asking the girl at the window about the price of her ticket and the time of arrival.

"So, what did the lady say?" Mom asked.

"The ticket was forty pesos and we will arrive at Puesta del Sol at 2:00 p.m. this afternoon," Nancy responded, rather pleased that this first attempt at communicating had gone well.

"Your suitcases are all aboard the bus," Dad announced as they joined the ladies.

"We saw to that," Joey added.

To cover a sudden flood of emotion, Nancy focused on her first use of Mexican money.

"I managed to understand everything and give the ticket girl the right amount of money," she sighed, feeling relieved.

The bus was pulling up for passengers to board.

"Take care, my girl," Dad's voice was gruff with emotion.

"I will! And God will take care of me too," she responded.

"I know," he smiled.

"We'll pray," Mom whispered.

As Nancy turned to Joey, he teasingly took a step backward. "None of this mushy stuff now."

Then, in a rush, his young arms were around her in a crushing bear hug. He released her, and she looked up at Dan.

"You'll come visit?"

"I will! Just let me know when."

"As soon as I'm settled in."

She stepped aboard the bus with a final wave and was soon seated. Seconds later as the vehicle pulled away, she felt herself moving toward a wondrous adventure with Jesus.

Chapter 2
Welcome

The swaying of the bus began to lull Nancy into a semi-consciousness. Though her excitement vied for attention, the stress of the last few days coupled with the emotion of departure won out, and she dozed off.

Sometime later she was startled into wakefulness by the bus driver's booming voice.

"Puesta del Sol, Puesta del Sol."

She sprang to attention filled with both anticipation and trepidation. They were already slowing to a stop.

"Dear Jesus, what should I do? How will I know where to go?

She signed with relief at the sight of someone, a lady, standing near the bus stop.

"I'll ask her." Nancy began to form in her mind the words she would use in Spanish, but before she could take the first step away from the bus, the lady came scurrying toward her with extended arms. "Hermana Nancy! Hermana Nancy!"

"She called me 'sister.' What a sweet greeting!"

By now those arms had engulfed Nancy, and the lady had planted a light kiss on her cheek. Though a little disconcerting at first, Nancy was to become very appreciative of the spontaneous affection her Mexican 'sisters' always expressed.

"I am Myra," the woman was saying. "We were expecting you and I'm so glad you have arrived safely. Look!" she pointed. "My husband is getting your baggage into his pickup. He will take it down to your house. We can walk. It's only a little way."

Myra caught herself at Nancy's puzzled look. "Oh! I'm so excited and talking way too fast!"

She slowed her rapid Spanish, trying to enunciate more clearly.

As they turned their steps down the sandy street, Myra chatted on enthusiastically. "We are going to be neighbors," she declared.

They were walking toward a group of adobe dwellings with beautiful blooms in their front patios. Myra guided Nancy toward one of the small houses. Nancy caught her breath at the four o'clocks lining the low wall around the patio. A pink climbing rose crept up the house wall to the window beside the door.

"Oh, Myra! It's lovely!" She exclaimed, forgetting she needed to use Spanish. She caught herself and put it all in one word, "Hermoso!"

Myra chuckled. "Do you like it?"

"Yes! Yes!" Nancy exclaimed and this time in her new language.

A smiling man, probably in his forties, jumped from the pickup parked nearby.

"I'm Enrique, Myra's husband," he announced offering his hand, "and you're our long-awaited Miss Nancy. You can't imagine how happy we are to have you here. We're your next door neighbors. So, if you need anything, it's just a holler across the fence you see. We're available day or night."

"Shall I carry your things inside?" Enrique went on.

"Oh, yes, please. When it comes to neighbors, I think I have..." she hesitated. She wanted to say, "prize winners" but she settled for "the best."

"Oh! It's frustrating," she fretted, "to not be able to say just what you want to express!"

She turned to Myra.

"Maybe I can find a teacher," again not knowing how to say 'tutor', "for my Spanish. I badly need one."

"You're doing very well," Myra smiled. "But, yes, I know just the one. I'm sure the school teacher over in the next village would be happy to work with you."

Enrique was calling from inside the house. "Miss Nancy, where would you like each of these suitcases?"

She stepped to the door of her new home to indicate where he might set kitchen items, bedding, books, etc. She thanked him gratefully when the task was finished.

"You must need some rest," Myra sympathized. "I'll help you make up your bed. But would you like a cup of coffee with us first?"

"Oh, yes! Thank you!" Nancy responded.

The hot coffee with a touch of cinnamon and rich goat's milk for cream was truly welcome.

Myra accompanied Nancy to help with the bed making but didn't linger.

"You rest!" she admonished. "I'll call you for some supper later and I'll help you with unpacking tomorrow."

Nancy searched her mind again for some appropriate words but just settled for a heartfelt, "Thank you! Thank you!"

She had not yet had time to look over her new little home until now. It had adobe walls, of course, and her floors were cement somehow smoothed to a shine. The rugs she had brought would make the room homey and comfortable. She peeked into the kitchen. Yes, that cupboard above the stove would do for her meager supply of dishes and pans.

"And this small refrigerator, I'm so thankful to have it. I'll have to get things to fill it tomorrow."

She opened the door and gasped. The shelves were full!

"Myra," she whispered. "She's thought of everything! What a dear friend to have already! Jesus, you've given me these gracious people. They've done everything to make me comfortable and welcome. Please show me how to spread your message of love here in Puesta del Sol."

She glanced at her watch.

"Mom is surely waiting for my call. So much has happened in these couple of hours, I have so much to tell her!"

She picked up her phone and dialed.

"Nancy! You're safely there. How are you, Dear?

"Oh Mom! I'm so blessed and helped!"

"Tell me. Did you find your way in the village? Was there someone to meet you?"

Nancy described in glowing detail Myra and Enrique's deeply appreciated welcome, their assistance with luggage, their invitation to coffee and to supper. "And we are next door neighbors, Mom."

"Where are you now?" came Mom's concerned question.

"Right here in my little house. It's cozy, Mom. The front is all living room. The back part is divided into the kitchen and my bedroom. And Mom! I have a small refrigerator filled with food: eggs, milk, cheese, tortillas, refried beans! I strongly suspect Myra has something to do with all of that. Why did I fret? God had every single item accounted for from the moment I stepped off that bus. Now, what about you? Dad and Joey? Did the day wear you out?"

"No, sweetie. We're fine. We miss you."

"Miss you, too. Thank you for your prayers. I love you."

After finishing her heartwarming talk with Mom, she let her body's clamor for respite take over. She snuggled against the comfy softness of her pillow and was soon asleep.

Nancy awoke just before Myra's call to supper. Her place at the table was the only one equipped with silverware. She watched her host and hostess skillfully scoop up their food with bits of tortilla and determined to learn to do that as gracefully as they.

After some conversation, Nancy paused at the door to express her gratitude and bid them a good night.

"Tomorrow," Myra offered, "the fruit and vegetable truck comes by. If you need anything, you'll hear his bell."

"Thank you, Myra. Thanks to both of you for everything."

She was anxious to call Dan and picked up the phone as soon as she closed her own door behind her.

Chapter 3

Grandma Victoria

Myra was in her patio when Nancy opened her own door next morning.

"How did you dawn?" came Myra's cheerful greeting.

The strange expression perplexed Nancy, but she was able to respond quickly. "Very well!" she smiled.

"I'll be over soon," Myra called.

In the meantime, Nancy reached for her Bible. She turned to Psalm 32 and caught her breath as she read verse eight.

"That's my answer, Jesus! You will 'instruct and teach me in the way that I should go. You will guide me!' Thank you! Thank you! Just help me follow your directions!"

She responded to Myra's knock and beckoned her into the kitchen. She'd carefully thought through the Spanish words she would use as she opened her refrigerator.

"I'm sure you know something about this," she hinted.

"Myra! Eggs, cheese, milk, tortillas, a mango!"

Myra laughed. "Just a few things. We don't want our new missionary to be losing weight!"

Nancy was overwhelmed! Tears came as she hugged this precious new friend. They turned to the mound of boxes, bags, and suitcases. Myra whistled as she peeked into Nancy's collection of books.

"You're going to need a bookcase. Enrique can build you one soon, I'm sure."

The next box contained Nancy's first aid and medical supplies.

"Oh, Nancy!" Myra exclaimed. "Would you have something in here for Grandma Victoria? Her mouth is full of canker sores. She can hardly eat."

Myra motioned as she talked and Nancy understood. She rummaged in the large box and came up with a bottle of vitamin E oil.

"This will soothe those sore spots," she said with satisfaction.

"Let's make her some pudding, too. It's smooth and cool. I'm sure she can enjoy it."

Opening another big box, Nancy found a package of instant vanilla pudding which she held up for Myra to see. Myra clapped her hands and they set to work preparing the treat. Nancy felt a surge of thanksgiving at these first efforts to communicate in Spanish and sent a silent prayer heavenward. With pudding and oil in hand, they began the steep climb to Grandma's home where she lived surrounded by her son, his wife, and their three stair-step little ones.

The children stared as Nancy was introduced to elderly Victoria. They soon threw their timidity to the wind however to crowd around this smiling "American." Surely, she needed to know all they could tell her about Grandma's sore mouth and how helpful they had been in taking care of her.

Nancy bent to their level trying desperately to catch the Spanish words that tumbled from three little mouths at once.

Their mother drew her chattering youngsters aside to express gratitude for the relief Nancy's remedies had brought her mother-in-law. Grandma was smiling and enjoying spoonfuls of cool pudding.

Promising to return soon, Myra and Nancy took their leave, waving "goodbye" to their three little neighbors perched on the patio fence. A few minutes later the two ladies sat down to their own dishes of cool dessert.

"Nancy," Myra began. "Saturday is September 16, Mexico's Independence Day. But we celebrate the night before. Do you think, with my help, you can be sufficiently settled in here so you can go with us to San Diego for the celebration?"

"Ready or not, I can't miss your Independence Day celebration," Nancy enthused.

"Our daughter lives in San Diego," Myra went on. "I'm anxious for the two of you to meet. If you can manage, we will go early and spend some time with her and Marco. They were married in June. He's the best! You'll enjoy them both."

"Oh, Myra! I'm getting excited! That will be so special to meet them and enjoy the celebration with all of you! I'll be ready!"

Nancy woke with a sense of excitement Friday morning. Today she would meet Myra and

Enrique's daughter and son-in-law! What an adventure to be here just in time for Mexico's celebration of independence. She made time to hurry up the hill to check on Grandma Victoria.

Hopefully, those "fires" in her mouth as they called them, were healing well.

"Oh, Miss Nancy! Miss Nancy!" Grandma called out as her benefactor came into view. Grandma was grinning from ear to ear.

"You are a miracle worker!"

"It wasn't I, Grandma," Nancy responded. "It was God, Himself, who loves you so much. He just had me here to help."

"I can eat, Miss Nancy! I can dance like the little miss at her fifteenth birthday party."

Grandma stood slowly, holding on to her cane, she did a few fancy steps on the sunbaked earth. Nancy laughed and gave Grandma a big hug. She turned to see the three little ones of the household coming to join the merriment. She knelt in front of the children to be on their level.

"Tell me your names," Nancy begged.

The oldest of the small girls responded. "I am Josefina, and he," turning toward her brother, "is Jose Luis. My little sister is Clarisa. That's a pretty name, don't you think?"

"And my name is pretty, too," Josefina went on, putting her small hand on her own chest. "And so is Jose Luis' name a pretty one."

"You are right! You all have pretty names," Nancy smiled.

"You are a very nice lady," Jose Luis broke in, speaking for the first time.

"I do hope so!" Nancy answered, "because I want to be like Jesus."

"Jesus?" Josefina queried.

"Jesus is God's Son, you know," Nancy explained. "And He loves you very much."

"He does? I'm glad!" the little girl beamed.

"Would you like to come to my house soon to see my pictures and hear a story about Jesus?"

"Yes! Yes!" the three children chorused.

"You'll need to ask your mama if it's alright." Nancy admonished.

This sent the youngsters scurrying toward the kitchen. Laura came to the door wiping perspiration from her forehead.

"Oh, Miss Nancy! Thank you for coming. I was just finishing my endless task of getting enough tortillas ready for this hungry family today. What are these little ones so excited about?"

Nancy explained and Laura agreed to the children's visit with her on Monday.

"I must get back," Nancy excused herself. "I'm going with Myra and Enrique to the Independence Day celebration in San Diego, but I did want to check on Grandma."

"We're so thankful for what you did, Miss Nancy. She is fine now. We were really concerned for her."

Chapter 4
Independence Day in Mexico

Afternoon found Enrique, Myra, and Nancy climbing into Enrique's pickup to start their trip to San Diego and the independence festivities.

Once seated, Myra began an account of Mexico's struggle for independence.

"We'll be honoring Miguel Hidalgo, Mexico's hero," she began her story. "It was way back in 1810 when a group of our people began secret meetings. Their hearts were crying out for liberation from decades of Spanish rule. A priest by the name of Miguel Hidalgo fostered and encouraged these efforts. As was bound to happen, the movement was discovered and Hidalgo's life was threatened. The rebels moved to a different area for their leader's safety, but his fervor could not be contained.

Defiantly, he tolled the church bell as his cry of 'Viva Mexico!' rang out. War erupted. The valiant man managed to escape his captors for a year, but he eventually paid with his life. A tragedy it was, but not in vain. His followers fought for eleven years until the Spaniards finally relinquished their hold and our freedom was a reality!"

"Eleven years!" Nancy exclaimed. "Imagine the heroism, the sacrifice! Thank you for your story! Now I can really appreciate Mexico's celebration."

Shortly after the account ended, Enrique was parking the pickup in front of a small stucco home on one of San Diego's quiet streets. Sonya, the couple's daughter, came running across the patio to greet her guests. She was so much like her mother, that same fond greeting, the animated "never know a stranger" chatter.

"Come in! Come in!" she invited. "Lunch is all ready."

Nancy had learned that "comida", meaning food, was a meal served somewhere between 2:00 and 3:00 in the afternoon. So, she had had a snack before leaving home. Now "food" sounded very good.

Marco also greeted his guests and proceeded to make them feel right at home in the living room. Sonya and her mother soon turned toward the kitchen, motioning for Nancy to follow. Mother and daughter attended to a few last-minute things for the meal. They refused Nancy's offer to help.

"No! No!" Sonya insisted. "You sit right there. We'll be eating in a moment. Then, you must tell us all about your 'mama' and 'papa', your sisters and brothers and how you came to Puesta del Sol."

"Everything smells delicious," Nancy commented as they sat down at the table.

"I hope you will like it," Sonya smiled.

The conversation was lively. Marco and Sonya had no end of questions for Nancy. She described home-life in Texas, her father's ranching, which was on a rather large scale compared to similar endeavors in Mexico. They registered surprise at hearing that Nancy had only one sibling to help in her father's undertaking

Their guest was tired, after a time, from the effort of putting all of this in Spanish. Coupled with the deep concentration she'd given Myra's story during the drive to San Diego, she was a little overwhelmed.

Marco's suggestion of a sightseeing tour of the town offered a welcome change. A real point of interest was the city plaza where the evening celebration would take place. Several men were occupied here and there, evidently arranging light displays. A few townsfolk strolled about the ample space between an elegant cathedral on one side and a rather ornate municipal building across the court. She noted the small balconies at each second-floor doorway adorned with banners for the evening.

"This will look quite transformed for tonight," commented Marco.

They drove by an extensive market.

"A good place for you to come Christmas shopping," Sonya suggested.

Marco drew the pickup to a stop beside a beautiful little park.

"Would you like to get out and walk around a few minutes?"

Everyone agreed. Trees, which must have witnessed eons of the city's history, shaded flowered areas. They stood by the pool where ducks and geese swam through the spray of a fountain. Children were laughing as they tossed bits of tortilla to the swimming fowls. Myra turned to her son-in-law.

"Marco, could we drop by the supermarket? I need a couple of things and maybe Nancy can find something she could use."

"Sure, let's go."

The size of the store and the variety it offered surprised Nancy. "How I'd like to have a small beef roast," she murmured. Turning to Myra, she asked about the right Spanish word to use in ordering the meat, but when she reached the indicated counter, she couldn't for the life of her remember if the term ended in an 'o' or an 'a'. She hurried to express her order to the waiting attendant and was teased good naturedly by the young man. She had asked for an octopus rather than her roast!

All in all, it was a learning experience, and the clerk had been kind enough not to over embarrass her. He cheerfully wrapped her roast. She tucked her purchase into her small ice chest as they headed back toward the young couple's home.

As Marco had said the city plaza was truly transformed when they entered the noisy crowd that evening. Nancy immediately spied an effigy of a man done in tiny lights. His features were ingeniously fashioned by a combination of red and white bulbs.

"That must be Miguel Hidalgo," she whispered to Sonya.

"You're right! How did you know about Miguel Hidalgo?"

"Your mother told me the story of independence on the way here," Nancy answered.

"She'd be the one to clue you in," Sonya laughed. "She's our historian."

"I love history, too," Nancy admitted. "I'm so happy I could be here tonight!"

"And we're happy to have you. We're so thankful you've come to strengthen the efforts for the Lord in Puesta del Sol. You're such an encouragement to my parents."

Marco and Sonya moved from cluster to cluster of celebrating San Diego citizens introducing Nancy as they went.

As they neared the opposite side of the plaza, Sonya suggested that they step into a small shop across the street.

"Let's treat Nancy to a trolley bus," she winked.

"Whatever is a trolley bus?" came Nancy's puzzled query.

"Come! You'll love it!" Sonya put her arm through Nancy's and led her into the tiny eating place.

Seated with the couples at a small table, she was given the choice of several pureed fruits poured over crushed ice.

"Mango sounds delicious," she decided.

That seemed to be the favorite of all.

A smiling waitress soon set frosty goblets of the refreshing treat in front of them.

"Umm! Wonderful!" Nancy exclaimed.

As they joined the crowd in the darkening plaza, Nancy's gaze fell on a row of low buildings along the opposite side of the huge area. They were covered with strings of tiny lights hung from roof to tiled walkway. Suddenly, those lights were being rapidly extinguished from roof top down, giving the effect of cascading water.

Nancy caught her breath. "How beautiful!"

Bands were beginning to fill the air with strains of Mexico's national anthem and other Mexican favorites. After a time, lights colored in the reds and greens of Mexico's flag, began to dance across the municipal building, calling attention in that direction. A spotlight targeted the center balcony. San Diego's mayor stepped into view. The crowd hushed as this dignitary raised his hand for attention. His voice boomed over the sound system.

"Viva Mexico!"

A roaring crescendo of response rose from the multitude below.

"Viva! Viva Mexico!"

The patriotism exuded by the celebrators made Nancy's heart pound with sheer thrill.

Bands again struck up the national anthem. And the crowd, still in holiday mood, began to wander slowly toward their nearby homes or to their vehicles. They soon found themselves at Marco and Sonya's front door.

"Are we going to have our prayer circle?" Sonya asked.

"Yes, of course," from Myra as they joined hands.

"Would you like to pray, Nancy? In English, if you wish."

"Alright," Nancy agreed. "English this time. But I promise it will be Spanish soon."

Nancy expressed her gratitude and delight for the eventful day and with final farewells they climbed into Enrique's pickup. The ride home was quiet and comfortable. They were all tired and contented after the long day's activities. Nancy bid them "Good night" at her door, and after an evening prayer, sank into the covers.

Saturday was filled with preparations for the next day. Enrique had asked her for a few words to introduce herself to the congregation next morning.

"It doesn't have to be long," he encouraged. She wrote and rewrote what she would say about her own Christian experience and God's leading that had brought her to Puesta del Sol. Then she proceeded to learn the short testimony word for word. She made a few changes using her Spanish dictionary and then went over her couple of paragraphs three more times.

He had also asked if she could give the children a Bible story. That wasn't so difficult. She had pictures of several Gospel narratives. She chose the account of Jesus and the children and put little notes in Spanish on the back of each picture in case she needed them.

Nancy did breathe a sigh of relief next morning when the service was over. Everyone had been so kind, congratulating her on her Spanish and giving expressions of gratitude for what her much needed help meant to the whole village.

She was quite exhausted after her own contribution to the service. She had also concentrated diligently on Enrique's morning message. It had all taken its toll.

After lunch, she was just dozing off when a frantic knock sounded at her door. Myra was there holding the hand of a sobbing little girl.

"Oh, Nancy!" Myra was breathless. "Lupita just fell here in the street. She's injured her knee quite badly. Can you help?"

"Of course!" Nancy was on her knees immediately checking the bloody wound.

"Come inside. We'll fix it right away."

She put an arm around the little girl.

"Sit here, Lupita. I'll wash your knee very carefully and we'll put on some medicine to soothe the pain. Then, we'll bandage it all up."

Lupita remained hesitant, but had stopped sobbing now. Nancy worked painstakingly to avoid any unnecessary discomfort for the child.

"There," she smiled when the last band-aid was in place. "Would you like a cookie?"

"Thank you," Lupita responded shyly. Then, very softly, "Miss, could I take one for my mother?"

"Oh, Lupita, how thoughtful of you! How many are in your family?"

"Well there's Mama and Papa and my two brothers and my little sister."

"Let's put a cookie for each of you in this plastic bag. Would you like that?"

"Oh, yes!" Lupita was smiling now.

Myra looked over Lupita to mouth her appreciation. "Thank you so much, Nancy."

"Come tomorrow, Lupita, if you would like me to change your bandage," Nancy offered at the door.

"I will!" the little girl responded.

Chapter 5
Clarisa Is Sick

"Clarisa's sick, Otoniel," Laura called.

She hated even to mention the little girl's fever and the hectic day she'd had. She knew her husband was dead tired after wielding his corn knife all day and stacking the stalks of corn. Bleary-eyed, he stood in the bedroom door.

"What's wrong?"

"She's been whimpering all day with this fever. I tried to cool her off with cloths dipped in the spring water but it didn't help much."

He came to stand over the child where Laura sat holding her. He felt her forehead.

"She is hot! Give her some of that medicine

we brought from San Diego. It helped the other two. She'll be better by morning."

"I'll try," Laura sighed. "She's hardly eaten all day. She just turns her head away. Go to bed, dear. I know you're worn out."

"Try to come soon."

"Alright. Good night."

But Laura didn't join her husband. She held the fussy youngster all night, desperately trying to think of something that would help. Clarisa refused the medicine. The cloths cooled in the water offered no help.

Toward morning, the little girl slept from sheer exhaustion. Laura dropped into bed still holding her sick daughter.

"How is she?" Otoniel stepped into the kitchen before sunrise next morning.

"About the same," Laura answered wearily as she poked the wood fire and set water on for coffee. She turned from the stove to face him. "Should I take her to Miss Nancy?"

He stepped closer so that other members of the household wouldn't overhear their conversation.

"I really don't want us to do that, Laura. Miss Nancy helped us so much when Mama had those sores in her mouth. I was very grateful. But we mustn't get more and more indebted to her. I've been thinking, we ought not to be letting the children go to her house for those stories on Mondays."

"Oh! Otoniel!" Laura protested.

"Think of it this way, Laura. Miss Nancy is a good person. She came here to help us when anybody is sick and she's done it, but she also came to share her way of thinking about God. We have our own religion, Laura. Someday she's going to ask us to that church down there. The more we become dependent on her, the more difficult it will be to say 'no.'"

At her despairing sigh, he drew her close. "We'll find a way. Talk with Mama. She has some good home remedies. She cured many a malady when I was growing up."

"I'll make her some chamomile tea," Grandma Victoria announced from the doorway, having heard Otoniel boast of her medicinal successes.

Grandma rocked and crooned and offered her "tried and true" remedies throughout the day, but the little one didn't respond. Evening came.

Laura said nothing to Otoniel as he sat propped on one elbow finishing the rice and beans she had prepared for his supper She watched him rise, sensing his weariness. Clarisa's illness weighed on him, too. He started toward the bedroom, then stopped and turned.

"Are you alright?"

She nodded, forcing a weak smile.

"Did Mama's medicine help?"

"She did her very best. She really did, but we've still not seen much change. Her fever hasn't left her at all."

"I've thought of catching the bus to San Diego with her, Laura, taking her to Dr. Canales, but you know how that is. I can't get a bus back here 'til the next morning. What would I do with my sick little girl all night in the bus station?"

"I know," she barely whispered. "Please go rest. You're so tired."

She sat numbly half dozing. She heard Otoniel's deep breathing. Minutes passed. Clarisa stirred in her arms. The whimper changed to a pitiful wail.

"No! No! My little one!" She lifted the child against her chest trying to comfort her and to muffle her cries. Laura's thoughts raced.

"This can't go on! I'm so scared!"

Her eyes rested on the lantern hanging from

its peg by the door.

"I'm going to Miss Nancy! I can't stand this any longer!"

She cautiously lowered the lantern to the table and lit the wick.

She pulled the door ajar and picked up her little girl. With a shawl around her shoulders and tucked around Clarisa's petite form, the lantern in hand, she slipped from the house.

Depending on the lantern's feeble help, Laura inched her way down the hill hoping against hope that Miss Nancy wasn't already asleep. A great sigh of relief escaped her lips as Nancy's lighted window came into view. Nancy was quick to answer this rather late unexpected knock at her door.

"Laura! What's wrong?" Her look of love and concern sent a billow of warmth and relief to encircle Laura. Placing the little girl in Nancy's outstretched arms, she burst into tears.

"Clarisa is so sick, Miss Nancy," she began between sobs. "I didn't know what to do."

Nancy laid the three-year-old on the blanketed bench which served as her sofa and guided Laura to a chair.

"Please, Laura, don't hesitate to come. This is my work, my calling. I want only to help when I'm needed. Tell me about it."

"She started yesterday morning with this fever and she refused to eat all day."

Nancy nodded, "Let me check her throat." Gently, she opened the little mouth just a bit.

With the help of her small medical lamp, she was able to catch a glimpse of the fiery redness in Clarisa's throat.

"She has a bad infection, Laura. I'll have to give her an injection. I'll be very careful," she added at Laura's look of concern.

There was a little shriek, but no tears as Nancy inserted and withdrew the needle.

"Would you hold her while I get some syrup and antibiotics for you to take home?"

A prayer of gratitude went up for her small refrigerator which provided the cool temperature some of her supplies needed.

"This syrup will soothe her throat and fight the fever. I'll give her some now and you can give her a spoonful in the morning. Put this little measure full of antibiotics in her 'atole.'" The smooth tasty Mexican porridge would be swallowed easily and the medicine never noticed.

"Now I am going to help you back up the hill. I will carry Clarisa and my flashlight. You bring the medicine and the lantern."

Laura's protests were to no avail. Nancy was already out the door.

Both were breathless when they stepped into Laura's kitchen.

"I think she will sleep now," Nancy reassured the exhausted mother.

She placed Clarisa in the rocker covering her with Laura's shawl. As she turned to say, "good night" Laura flung her arms around Nancy's shoulders.

"What would we have done if you hadn't been here!" she whispered. "Thank you! Thank you! Maybe when harvest is over, we can repay you somehow."

"Laura, Jesus sent me here to help. That is what I want to do. That is all the payment needed. Please get some good rest now. I'm sure Clarisa will be improved by morning."

And she was!

"Laura," Otoniel called. "Clarisa is sitting up and asking for something to eat."

He appeared in the bedroom doorway with his daughter in his arms.

"See, I told you Mama's remedies could work miracles."

He seated Clarisa at the table and poured her a little milk. His wife said nothing. He glanced at her sober face. Where was that smile of joy and relief? Hadn't she heard him?

"Otoniel," she began. "I took Clarisa down to Nancy last night." She hurried on. "I held her here after you were asleep. The whimpering turned into a feeble wail. I was so scared!"

"You carried her down that hill in the dark?" he whispered, incredulous.

"I took the lantern," she countered. "I didn't know what else to do!" Her eyes were filled with tears. "Please, don't be angry!"

He stretched out his arms to her. "Come here." She clung to him sobbing.

"It's alright! It's alright!" he soothed.

Finally, the crisis was over. He dabbed clumsily at her tear-stained cheeks with his red handkerchief.

There was something else nagging at Laura's mind as well.

"Otoniel, if we keep the children from going down to Nancy's story time, what can I tell her?"

"I've been thinking about that. I really could use some help in the field, Laura. Corn ears are scattered across the rows where they fell as I was

46

cutting. Jose Luis and Josefina could gather them up while I husk and then carry ears to the wagon.

If you could spare a little time to help husk? Mama can handle things in the kitchen, and," turning to the child at the table, "you can help Grandma, can't you, Clarisa?"

The little girl's eyes brightened. "Yes! Yes! I can help Grandma a lot!"

So, it was settled. The children and Laura would be needed to help with the harvest. There just wouldn't be time to go to Nancy's house on Monday afternoons.

Chapter 6
Dan's Visit

Dan stepped a little hesitantly from the bus looking toward the small station and along the street. Where was Nancy? He had thought she would surely be right here to meet him.

"Hola, Gringo!" A pleasant looking man extended his hand with a smile. Then, slowly and in careful English, "I can help you?"

"Nancy Jefferson," Dan responded overly-agitated.

"Oh, Miss Nancy, come!" The man motioned Dan to follow.

They walked in silence the short distance to a small adobe house where the gentleman knocked.

There was no response.

"Myra," the man called. "Do you know where Nancy is?"

An attractive Mexican lady appeared at the door of the next house.

"She went to La Mesa for the children's meeting and her Spanish class with Miguel but she should have been back some time ago."

Dan was none the wiser for all this conversation in Spanish. Just at this moment Nancy herself appeared running up the incline from the creek just beyond the houses.

"Oh, Dan!" she gasped breathless from her sprint up the short rise.

"I'm so sorry! The car--" she stopped to catch her breath.

"What happened?" Dan interjected, his concern pressing for the explanation.

"Well, the car slid a little on the bridge over the creek. It rained just enough to make the bridge slippery. My VW ran into the bank. We had to get the oxen to pull it on up the incline. The fender is bent but Miguel, my Spanish coach, is working on it now."

"Are you alright?"

"Yes, yes! I wasn't hurt at all."

Dan hadn't expected to arrive at a moment of crisis in this unfamiliar place. It was a little unsettling to say the least. Enrique stood patiently waiting for Nancy's explanation in Spanish. She turned to him now apologetically.

"Alright," he responded to her account. "I'll go see if I can help Miguel."

"I didn't mean for your arrival to be so hectic. Come sit down."

She indicated a wooden bench shaded by a newly erected shelter beside her front door. It wasn't long before Enrique came, parking her car in its place and bringing her the keys.

"All fixed," he assured her.

"Thank you so much, Enrique! Miguel?"

He's on his way with his 'critters', Enrique smiled. "See you later."

"May I ask some questions?" Dan took up the conversation.

"Of course! I'll answer if I can."

"Where do you buy food here? Is there some sort of store?"

Nancy explained about the weekly fruit and vegetable truck and promised a trip to San Diego to see the supermarket there.

"I brought you a few things from home," he said pointing at the bag beside him.

"Oh, Dan! Thank you! You're so thoughtful. I know I'll enjoy whatever you brought."

"Your mom's special bread for one thing," he smiled.

"Yum! Yum!" said Nancy. "Any other questions?"

"And where do you get good water here?"

"There are springs just behind the village." She pointed. "You can see the rock formations from here. There is a supply of water for the whole village as well as the cattle. Why don't we walk over there? Would you like to? I'll bring my pitcher."

"Yes, let's go for a walk."

It was a companionable stroll through green pasture to the pool where a few animals were quenching their thirst. Nancy pointed to sparkling water gushing from crevices in the rock wall, "It's pure and good. I'll fill my pitcher before we leave."

They stood a few minutes just enjoying the peaceful scene of the pool, the animals, the mist rising from the rushing water, and the late afternoon sun.

Nancy glanced at her watch. "Oh, it's nearly time. We're invited to Enrique and Myra's for supper."

At his questioning look, she added, "Her meals are just wonderful. Maybe she has made flan. It's a delicious custard topped with a caramel sauce."

After enjoying Myra's steaming chicken and rice dish, as well as the hoped-for flan dessert, Dan asked Nancy to question Enrique about his farming. Enrique rose from the table beckoning Dan to follow. They leaned on the back-patio fence as Enrique pointed to his fourteen black and white milk cows just heading back to pasture. Several goats bounced along with the cattle. Dan chuckled as the frisky animals seemed to play a game of leapfrog, bounding over one another. Enrique motioned Dan to a small garden plot. He did a hoeing motion but pointed toward the house indicating that this was Myra's project. They stepped into a toolshed where a great amount of some plant fiber was hung to dry in small bunches. Dan gave Enrique a questioning look. To this, his host responded by pointing out a piece of rope which it was quite evident had been made from the fibers. Some fiber was boxed and ready. Dan imagined it would be sold as another source of income.

As they entered the house again, Myra led Dan to a small room. Asking Nancy to translate, she explained that they were more than happy for him to occupy their recently married daughter's vacant bedroom. He smiled his gratitude and after walking Nancy to the door, he returned for some much needed rest. Myra handed him a basin of warm water with a towel and bid him good night.

Nancy was at Myra's door next morning when Dan emerged.

"Breakfast on the patio," she announced. "I'd like to introduce you to Grandma Victoria when we finish eating," she went on.

"Good!" Dan agreed. "She sounds like quite a fascinating little old lady from your phone calls. I'd really like to meet her as well as those three little grandkids you talk about."

Grandma's welcoming voice announced their arrival on the hill.

"Oh! Oh! Miss Nancy is bringing her sweetheart," she began teasing.

"No! No! Grandma! This is Dan. He is my friend, a wonderful friend of my family."

Nancy colored a little, thankful that Dan didn't understand.

Grandma turned to Dan. "Welcome to Puesta del Sol! I do hope you very much enjoy your visit. And has this fine young lady told you what she did for me when my mouth was full of 'fire'?"

Nancy laughed. "Slowly Grandma!" She was having difficulty keeping up with the translating.

At that moment the three small family members burst from the kitchen door to swarm about this tall white man's feet.

Grandma chuckled. "You have three good friends already."

Dan reached into his pocket for the little rolls of candy tucked in just for this anticipated meeting.

Clarisa was tugging at Dan's pant leg.

"I think she wants you to pick her up," Nancy whispered.

He lifted the child to nestle in his arms.

"You're a pretty man," Clarisa announced stroking his cheek with her tiny fingers.

"What's she saying?" he wanted to know.

"I think she's saying you are a nice man and good looking, too." Nancy filled in.

Having briefly chatted with the children's parents, Nancy and Dan bid farewell. Dan set Clarisa on the ground and patted her gently. The children followed to where the path turned downhill and Otoniel called them back. With a final wave, their visitors disappeared.

"Will they be in church tomorrow?" Dan asked.

"I don't think so, but I'm trying my best to befriend and encourage them. The children have come to my house for a few Bible stories."

"I'm so proud of you, Nancy. You're winning the hearts of these people."

"Thank you, Dan. We have time enough before lunch to drive to La Mesa if you'd like. You could meet the children from my Bible class and see Miguel and his mother."

"Great! Let's go!"

Nancy guided her blue VW toward the bridge where the slight accident had occurred the previous day.

"Nancy! Where are you going?"

"La Mesa is just a short distance beyond the bridge," she explained puzzled at his sudden reaction.

"But that bridge has no side rails! Yesterday the car slid on that bridge!"

"I've crossed it many times, Dan."

"You could have disappeared in this chasm and no one would have known!"

Nancy had to giggle at Dan's exaggerated term for the relatively shallow creek bed.

Dan was serious. "Isn't there another way?"

"Well, yes," Nancy admitted. "About a mile down there is a better bridge. It's just that you have to drive back a mile on the other side," she smiled apologetically.

"Will you please promise me that you'll use that bridge from now on?"

"I promise, Dan, so you won't be worried."

"Thank you!" He breathed relief.

La Mesa was a picturesque village nestled against an outcropping with a flat top from which the little town took its name. The children came running at the appearance of the now easily recognized blue car.

"Toot the horn!" they shouted. Nancy complied and they burst into laughter.

"Is it story time?" queried several of the youngsters.

"Not today," Nancy answered them. "But I will be sure to be here on Tuesday."

Miguel's mother appeared at the door of a nearby dwelling and hurried out to meet Nancy and her guest. They were immediately ushered in, and in true Mexican style, soon served steaming coffee and a plate of "empanadas". They both enjoyed the fruit-filled pastry.

Miguel soon entered to greet them enthusiastically. He had many comments on Nancy's progress in Spanish.

"We're so fortunate to have Miguel here with us," his mother explained. "He finished normal school last spring. Each normal graduate spends at least his first year teaching in one of the villages. To our joy, he was assigned right here."

"Miguel," Nancy requested. "Would you like to show Dan some of the pictures we took of your students and your classroom?"

Nancy explained as Miguel passed each picture. "He has kindergarten through fifth grade and teaching tools are somewhat limited. He makes up for it with his vivid explanations and his drawings. Those children are learning. I've sat in on his classes a couple of times," she added.

Nancy had a trip to San Diego in mind for the afternoon. She wanted Dan to see for himself the abundant source of necessities near at hand.

They thanked Miguel's mother for her hospitality, bid Miguel goodbye and were on their way.

"So, is this young man a real help with your Spanish?"

"Yes, he is. Having prepared to teach, he's good with grammar and I've learned a lot of vocabulary. He's very patient. I do make some terrible mistakes. Sometimes he laughs 'til the tears come."

"And how could it be so funny?" Dan wanted to know.

"Well, for example," Nancy cited a recent error.

"We were studying the face. I called the lips 'lobos'. Doesn't that make sense? We have earlobes. Couldn't lips be 'lobos'??"

"What does 'lobos' mean then?"

"Wolves," she admitted sheepishly. Dan grinned.

"While we're on the subject I might as well tell you, another slip I made. Miguel brings it up now and then and laughs again.

This time it's about 'ribs' which are 'costillas'. I most innocently called them 'cosquillas' which is 'tickles'. Quite appropriate, don't you think?"

Dan's grin widened and he began to chuckle.

"You're as bad as Miguel!" she pouted.

"But it is funny." She burst into laughter, too.

"Would you like to drive my little car to the

city?" Nancy asked. "We can pick up a hamburger on the way and have a real meal in town later."

"Sounds great!" Dan agreed.

The stop at San Diego's supermarket was an eye opener for Nancy's visitor.

"Are we really in Mexico? This looks almost like home."

It isn't much different, is it?"

As they passed the meat counter Nancy recounted her octopus story.

Dan raised his eyebrows.

"You actually ordered octopus?"

"Another of my boo boos. They just teased me a little bit and wrapped my roast. Sadly, my slip-ups continue, but it makes for fun. Myra wants us over for breakfast tomorrow morning so we need to pick up a bag of sweet rolls for her and a kilo of sugar. Then, are you hungry for some more yummy Mexican food?"

"Starving," Dan admitted.

They drove on to stop in front of the restaurant which Nancy claimed offered the best tacos in the entire world.

Plates arrived attractively arranged. Bits of lettuce, tomato and white cheese peeped from crispy taco shells. Dan noticed the pudding-like serving of something with a pinkish-brown hue.

"What am I eating?" he questioned as he lifted a mouthful to his lips.

"Those are mashed pinto beans which have been fried a little. They're yummy."

"I agree," he murmured savoring the tasty bite.

"And now for dessert," Nancy announced as they rose from their table.

She guided Dan through the streets pointing out the square where the Independence Day celebration had taken place.

He pulled the VW to a stop in front of the small restaurant she indicated.

Their fruity trolley buses were a perfect ending to the long day and the faithful blue car was soon purring toward Puesta del Sol.

"Talk about a perfect day, Nancy. This has been one of them," Dan announced as they turned toward the village.

"Really, Dan? I'm so thankful!"

"And I believe the sunset is going to add the final touch." He pointed to the western horizon.

"Oh, let's stop and walk over there, where the mountains and the cacti are silhouetted against the sky," Nancy exclaimed. She was out of the car almost before he pulled up.

"I did intend to stop!" he chided her teasingly.

"Let's not miss a moment of this sunset. It reminds me of home and the gorgeous dawns I see from my upstairs window. My tangerine sky!" Nancy babbled on tripping over the ridge of sod at the roadside.

Dan caught her elbow to steady her. They picked their way between cactus plants and shrubs and stood captivated by the glowing close of a beautiful day.

After a few moments, Nancy couldn't remain silent.

"Sometimes I compare God's tangerine skies to Noah's rainbow," she began. "No, it's not to reassure me of this year's appointment. I know this is right but the beauties of sunrises and sunsets are so special. They speak to me of His love, His care, His perfect plan for our lives."

"And you are sharing His love and care with these people, Nancy. You've already made so many friends and an impression for God in their lives."

"Oh, I hope so! Pray for me, Dan."

"I do, every day."

"Thank you!"

Light was fading. They turned toward the car.

"It's a little rough going here. Maybe we'd just better hang on to one another. We don't want to fall into a cactus," Dan suggested. He took her hand. It was good to have his support.

"Breakfast then about 8:30, Dan. The morning service starts at 10:00. After that, Enrique and Myra will be coming over. It's about my turn to cook, so you'll see my little home tomorrow."

To be very proper and respectful of the village people's principles, Dan had not set foot inside Nancy's small house.

"See you in the morning then. Would you put Myra's rolls and sugar on her table as you go in? Thank you! Good night."

Dan peeped through the door to Myra's kitchen. All was hushed. Evidently, the couple had just retired. He saw his pan of warm water placed on the stand beside his guest room door.

He did dread leaving tomorrow. He'd never been a stranger here. It was like they had known him forever and welcomed his visit. Puesta del Sol had won his heart. He turned a little sadly toward his bedroom.

Next door, Nancy quickly prepared her roast for the crockpot. It could cook all night. She'd add vegetables in the morning and fix a quick salad of the fruit cocktail, marshmallows, and coconut Dan had brought.

"It won't be a fancy meal but, hopefully, tasty and sufficient," she murmured.

She went over her children's story for tomorrow once again and then knelt beside her bed. Gratitude for Dan's visit, tomorrow's needs, her parents, and Joey were all lifted to the Lord. She slipped between the sheets.

Dan slid reluctantly into his bus seat next afternoon. How proud he'd been of Nancy in the morning church service. She had held the rapt attention of several little wigglers with her illustrated story of Jesus feeding the five thousand. And all in Spanish.

She'd made it possible for him to follow Enrique's message with little notes in English on a notepad. Dinner at her kitchen table with Enrique and Myra was a special finale to the whole visit.

Then they had walked to the bus station. There had been but a few moments to say goodbye.

"The time here has been unbelievable, Nancy," he said. "You're safe among Christian friends who love you. I do miss you but I know now that this is right."

"I'm so thankful! Thank you for coming. I miss you, too. But," she'd brightened, "Christmas isn't so far away. Bye, 'til then."

He watched her retreating figure now. The bus began to move. She turned and waved.

Chapter 7
Natalia's Papa

Nancy glanced up the hill once more, longing to see three small figures skipping and bounding toward her. They had always come bubbling with excitement for the Jesus story but not again today!

How long would it take to finish the corn harvest? And why this sudden reserve in Laura? It hurt her feelings. She decided to talk with Myra about it.

Soon, Lupita arrived with her brothers and small sister. She had brought along a friend as well today. Nancy forced herself to brighten up as she stepped inside the house matching the mood of the children. They were clamoring for their favorite chorus. She smiled at her little group as she took her seat.

"Before we sing, Lupita, could you introduce the friend you brought along today?"

"Oh! Yes!" Lupita blushed. "I forgot! This is Natalia. She's my cousin."

"Welcome, Natalia. We're very glad you're here."

"Thank you, Miss Nancy," the little girl responded. "I wanted to come last week and the week before that but I couldn't... but today I could!"

"Then, let's sing so Natalia can learn our chorus."

Nancy began the Spanish lyrics. "There's no other God like you." The children joined in.

"No, not one can do what you can do."

"That's exactly what our Jesus story is about today," Nancy announced. She opened her Bible and laid it across her lap.

"We all know how unhappy we feel when someone is sick at our house, don't we? If it's a sister or brother we can't play together. We can't make a lot of noise because the sick one has to rest. Maybe we just want to put our head in our hands and be sad."

Nancy demonstrated the dejected pose.

"When Jesus was here on earth, I believe there was a man who felt just like that." she went on.

"He had a very special servant who helped him every day. I imagine he brought the man his food, ran errands for him, did everything the master wanted or needed done. They were dear friends, the two of them.

"Then the servant got terribly sick. The master called the doctor and did everything possible to help his servant get well but the servant didn't get better and his master felt so, so bad.

"Right in the midst of his sadness, something marvelous happened. He heard about Jesus. He sent quickly to find the Lord Jesus, pleading for Him to make this dear servant well.

"Do you think Jesus was willing to do that? Of course, He was! Back at the master's house the servant's pain suddenly went away. I'm sure he called out all excited, 'Come! I don't hurt anymore!'

He must have got up from his bed. He felt well. He felt strong. He was amazed! 'Master,' he called. 'I'm well!'

"I'm sure the master came running to hug his dear servant. And I'm sure he was so very thankful to Jesus for making his servant all better.

"Let's have our prayer now. Just like the man who begged Jesus to heal his sick servant, we can always pray to him for help in whatever we need." Natalia's hand shot up.

"Miss Nancy, can we pray for my papa? He hurts so much!"

"Yes, yes, Natalia, we can pray for your papa. Can you tell us why he is hurting so?"

"Well, those big red ants, the ones that have mouths that look like claws, they bit him yesterday when he was working in the field. He has big red bites here and here and here. He hurt so much last night that he couldn't sleep."

"We are going to pray for him and I think I have some medicine that will help."

The children bowed their heads and earnestly joined in Nancy's prayer.

While the youngsters snacked on milk and cookies, Nancy packaged an ointment and some pain pills for Natalia's papa.

They started down the sandy street toward Natalia's home. The little girl clasped Nancy's hand.

"You know," she confided. "I'm sure it was Jesus who helped me come today. My papa needs those pills so much. Jesus knew that, didn't He?"

"Yes, He did know, Natalia, and He is answering

our prayer."

"And, Miss Nancy, Jesus sent you here, too, because if you weren't here there would be no pills." Nancy's eyes misted.

"Yes, Natalia, Jesus knew and planned it all. Aren't we thankful!"

"This is where I live," Natalia pointed.

They were met by Natalia's mother who gratefully accepted the medications. She rummaged in a small wooden box on the table and brought out a few pesos. Nancy declined but the lady insisted.

"Thank you then. I'll use them to buy more pills," Nancy agreed.

"Miss Nancy," Natalia's mother ventured. "We've been talking of going to church ever since you came. My nieces and nephews have been attending your Jesus story time. They love it and tell us all about it. I think we will see you Sunday. And thank you so much for the medicine."

Nancy bid them goodbye.

"Until Sunday then and we'll be praying for your husband."

She turned her steps quickly toward home to retrieve the last act of the Christmas play she had finished translating. She wanted Myra's suggestions and corrections. With Myra's comments, a few suggestions and a change or two in wording, all was ready for tomorrow's get together with the Christmas committee.

"You've done a fabulous job," Myra complemented Nancy. "I'm getting excited! This play has a real message. We'll need to pray for many to attend and take this to heart."

"Could we pray together right now, Myra? I'm so concerned about Laura and Otoniel. The children haven't come to story time for three weeks. And Laura is always occupied when I go. She makes excuses. I don't understand."

"I think it's mostly Otoniel, Nancy. I believe he's afraid, afraid to admit there is a Savior he needs to open his heart to and afraid of ridicule among the other men. Yes, let's pray for them and for our Christmas services."

Chapter 8
Christmas Play and Shopping Day

Nancy stepped across the patio and into her own living room with a lighter heart. As she woke next morning, the Scripture Myra had pointed out during their afternoon prayer time was echoing in her thoughts.

"I called unto the Lord, and He heard me." Had she been remembering that? He hears! They had prayed fervently for Otoniel and Laura. They had laid their Christmas plans in God's hands and He had listened!

She began to sing, "'Tis so sweet to trust in Jesus, just to take Him at His word." As she began her morning devotions, she thanked Him gratefully for his faithfulness even when she had been letting the problem become a mountain of fretting. She had let it overshadow the fact that though she hadn't seen the answer she so longed for, He was listening. The answer would come.

A light tap at the door reminded Nancy that it was time for their meeting with the other members of the Christmas committee. She joined Myra on the short walk to the church.

They were greeted by two older ladies. Dona Antonia had volunteered to be costume creator and Dona Beatriz, with the help of her teenage grandsons, would be responsible for scenery. The four found a comfortable place around a table at the back of the church.

"Now let's hear this new play!" Dona Antonia enthused.

"Alright," Myra agreed. "Nancy has translated the whole three acts."

"With great help from this lady." Nancy patted Myra's shoulder.

"Oh, not that much," Myra chuckled. "But listen now and give us your comments."

At the conclusion of the reading both ladies burst into applause and exclamations of approval.

"That's just precious, Mi Hijita!" (pronounced *E-he-tah*) Dona Beatriz reached an arm around

"Well, if you put it that way," Sonya called back, already halfway to her bedroom to pick up her purse and a shawl.

Sonya's acquaintance with every nook and cranny of the market place made shopping a cinch.

"An embroidered dress for your mama? Right this way." And Sonya forged ahead through the crowd of bustling shoppers.

Nancy was delighted with the gorgeous gowns, bright with rich embroidery.

"Let's see! Rose or turquoise? She'd love either one."

Nancy pondered but finally had the clerk bag the pretty turquoise dress.

"There's beautiful jewelry just around the corner if you're interested," Sonya announced.

On and on they went. By noon, all three were loaded down with their purchases. Nancy had found a lovely pendant to go with mom's dress, shirts and tooled billfolds for Dad, Joey and Dan, and caramel sauce which both Myra and Sonya recommended for ice cream topping. The other two were similarly burdened.

"Joey will disown me if I don't take blankets for Champ and Goldie," Nancy confided.

They have some good quality blankets toward

the back of the market," Sonya responded.

"But how about putting all of this in the car first?" she laughed. "We'll make better headway without all these bundles."

The guard on the street was more than happy to keep a watchful eye on the car and their purchases. Sonya rewarded him amply for his services.

Their appetites were demanding attention as they wound up their second trip into the marketplace. Nancy had decided on some wonderfully warm and attractive blankets for the family bedrooms, as well as protection from the chill for hers and Joey's favorite mounts in the stable.

Lunch was very welcome and tasty as usual.

"We really need to go by the supermarket yet," Myra suggested. "You'll need a box of Grandma's Hot Chocolate for your Christmas Eve around the tree."

"Is everybody up to this?" Nancy queried looking over her faithful guides for signs of wilting.

"Yes! Yes! Of course!" from both ladies.

The supermarket yielded the hot chocolate ingredients plus several confections Nancy's enthusiastic companions recommended.

"We want to send these to your family ourselves," Myra and Sonya declared. "They're just a small remembrance from those who love you here."

Nancy was deeply touched again by the spontaneous affection of these dear people God had sent her to.

"Can you come back to the house awhile?" Sonya asked hoping for an affirmative response.

Myra turned to Nancy.

"Love to," she smiled. "What a wonderful day!"

She put an arm around each, giving them a warm hug.

"I'll be thinking of this shopping trip over and over again!"

Within the week she would be heading to the Texas border and to her family for the holidays. Myra had insisted that she spend Christmas Eve at home.

"But the play, Myra, and all that needs to be done," she'd argued.

"You think we can't handle it!" Myra had teasingly puckered her lips in an assumed pout.

"Of course, you can!" came Nancy's affirmation

with a smile at Myra's pose. "But I want to hear all about it the moment I get back."

Chapter 9
Anticipation

"Joey wants to talk with you," Mom announced when Nancy dialed on Friday.

"Hey Nance," came the boyish voice. Then, in carefully enunciated syllables, "Como esta usted?"

"Well, you linguist!" Nancy laughed.

"And that's not all I know how to say," Joey hurried to inform her.

"Alright! Let me hear more of your Spanish communications."

"Well, I can ask directions to anywhere I want to go. I can say 'Where is the supermarket? Where is the ice cream shop? Where is the gas station?' I'm driving now, you know," he hastened to add.

"But this is the Spanish question I like best."

"And what is that best one?" Nancy waited.

There was a clearing of his throat. "Now listen carefully. Where did you hide my Christmas presents?"

Nancy laughed. "That, my young friend, will not be answered in Spanish or in English, until they are under the tree on Christmas Eve but let me tell Mom about my plans for arriving there with all these presents you are anticipating. She can share the answers to questions with all of you."

Mom Jefferson took up the phone again.

"I need to tell you," Nancy began, "what I'm hearing from Myra. She insists that I leave in time to celebrate Christmas Eve with my family."

"That's great, sweetheart!" Mom exclaimed. "Then you will be coming on Saturday?"

"Yes! The bus gets in about noon. I'm so excited!"

"We will be there! I can just hardly wait to see you, my dear! Please tell Myra how very much we appreciate her thoughtfulness."

"I will, Mom. See you soon!"

The days and hours flew by, one more Christmas practice, the trip to La Mesa to help Miguel with his program, popcorn balls to make for church folks and for Laura's family. She'd hardly seen them lately. She missed Grandma's sweet humor and festive spirit.

"And, please, Heavenly Father," she whispered. "I so want to enjoy a visit with Laura without this strange wall that for some reason has risen between us."

As Nancy spent hours making popcorn balls for the entire church family, she couldn't help but smile over the conversation with Joey… driving, getting so grown up… but still a little boy.

"Thank you, Jesus, for sending him into our lives. He is one of my greatest joys. How I miss him!"

Her thoughts wandered. "Would it be possible to bring him back with her for a few days after Christmas? No, that wouldn't work. Hmm… how about his spring vacation? What would Myra think?"

"Oh, Nancy, I love the idea!" Myra gushed. "He could have Sonya's room like Dan did. No! I think he'd be more comfortable there with you. We can take the bed over."

"Do you think he'd fit in with the boys here? He doesn't speak much Spanish."

"Of course, he would. They'd love having your brother here. They'd teach him enough words to play soccer," Myra laughed. "We'll have a ball!"

"Well, we'll talk it over at home during Christmas then."

Nancy tried to quell the excitement that was beginning to explode inside. Would this really be possible?

Only hours were left before she'd say goodbye to Puesta del Sol for a short week. She was bursting with happiness and yet regretting the separation from everyone here at this special time.

She just had to see Laura before leaving.

"I'll make them popcorn balls like all the rest and take Grandma Victoria my last package of instant pudding," she planned. "Oh! That Laura will be her old self and that we can have a good time together. Please, Jesus."

Laden with her yummy popcorn balls, a little tub of canned peaches for Grandma and the instant pudding, Nancy began the short trek up the hill. "Jesus," she whispered, "please go up there ahead of me and knock on the door of Laura's heart."

As Nancy topped the hill, Laura was just stepping through her kitchen door. Her cry of surprise and delight immediately reassured the hesitant visitor. They met halfway across the sunbaked patio with a warm hug.

"Oh! I'm so happy you've come. I miss you!"

With an arm about Nancy's shoulder, she directed their steps toward the kitchen door. "Come in for some coffee."

Inside Laura turned to place cups on the table. Nancy noted the half-hidden motion as her friend hastily brushed at her misty eyes but when she sat down across the table, tears flowed.

"I've missed you so much!" her words coming in little gasps of regret. "I wish I could explain. We have been busy," she sighed.

"It's alright, my dear friend. I think I understand. I've missed you, too. Let's just enjoy this time together. And to brighten the moment," she went on, "I brought you a bag of my special popcorn balls for all of you."

"The little ones will be home from school right away. They'll wake Clarisa and those three will be one circus when you mention popcorn balls."

Nancy laughed. "It will be so good to see those sweeties. By the way, where is Grandma Victoria?"

"She's resting," Laura sighed. "She just doesn't have much energy. I wish we could find something to help."

Her voice trailed off as Grandma herself appeared at the bedroom doorway.

"Miss Nancy!" Grandma Victoria's face broke into a welcoming grin. "I thought I was having a dream but here you are as real as ever!"

Grandma shuffled a little as she moved toward the table. She grasped Nancy's hand tightly as she seated herself alongside her.

"Coffee, Grandma?" Laura asked.

"Yes, Dear. Thank you," the older lady responded.

The door burst open with a shout from Jose Luis and Josefina who were very soon munching Nancy's treats with typical after school enthusiasm.

Clarisa appeared sleepy eyed from her nap but how those eyes brightened as Josefina held out a tempting popcorn ball.

"Nancy, I have something to show you," Laura announced as she disappeared through the bedroom door. She reappeared with a basket full of crocheted doilies in an array of vivid colors.

"I've been making these and thinking of you. Please choose some for yourself and take a couple you think your mother would like."

"Laura, they're beautiful! What a lot of work!"

"It's relaxing to sit down and crochet awhile after the day's work is done. I enjoy mixing and matching the colors," Laura responded.

Nancy chose two bright doilies for herself and two for Mom Jefferson in her favorite colors.

"Thank you, Laura. These are very special." Bidding them goodbye at the door amidst hugs from Grandma and the children, Nancy motioned for Laura to follow her outside.

"I'll get Grandma a good multivitamin on this trip north. If she's not better when I get back we'd best see Dr. Canales."

Chapter 10
Home for Christmas

The bus was a little late. Nancy strained to see the parking lot as they crept into the border station. There they were in the farm truck with Joey sitting jauntily at the wheel. Nancy began waving from the bus window. They were out of the truck and racing toward her in an instant. Mom reached her first.

"Oh, my dear! You look wonderful! Wonderful to your mama who has missed you so much!"

Dad grasped one of her hands and she flung her other arm around Joey. They stood in a great family hug with everyone talking at once.

"Your luggage, Miss," the bus driver interrupted.

"Oh, yes! Thank you!" She checked to see that each piece had arrived safely. Then, with everyone carrying bundles or a suitcase, they hurried merrily to the waiting truck. After passing through customs they were homeward bound.

Monday was a hubbub of readying everything for Christmas Eve. Mom and Nancy chatted and cooked while Joey offered to taste every dish to be sure it passed inspection as well as satisfying his ever-ready appetite.

Dan, having no family of his own, was always included in the Jefferson's festivities. He arrived in time to help Dad and Joey finish farm tasks early for the evening celebration.

The sound of soft carols filled the house as the family gathered. The results of Mom's and Nancy's hours in the kitchen met everyone's enthusiastic approval at the festive table. The clamor for "just one more spoonful" subsided into sighs of regret when passed dishes had to be ignored with "I can't take one more bite."

The men insisted that the cooks relax by the tree in the living room while they tidied up the kitchen.

Joey's loudly announced, "Present time!" brought everyone to find a comfortable chair by the tree with its mound of waiting gifts to be opened. Dad picked up the Bible to read the story, old but always new, of the birth in Bethlehem. The familiar words brought a reverent hush over the room. Dad's voice led out in a prayer of gratefulness for God's gracious blessings this night of family reunion to celebrate Jesus' birth.

Then Joey strode to the heaped packages beneath the tree. One finger at his cheek, he studied the tempting array before him. Choosing a gift, he carried it to Mom Jefferson.

"How beautiful!"

"Just your color."

"Put it on!" were the admiring comments as Mom held up the brightly embroidered dress Nancy had chosen from the San Diego market. Mom hurried to the bedroom to reappear dancing and delighted in her new attire.

The men's shirts were received with equal admiration and with the same cry of "Put them on!" Cameras flashed as the group reassembled around the tree. Joey greeted the saddle blanket for Champ with a whoop of joy. Mom was thrilled with gifts from Laura, Myra and Sonya.

Nancy blinked back tears as her lap filled with so many items she had lacked these first months in Puesta del Sol. She hadn't been able to take several small kitchen tools which would be so useful. Three pretty tops from Mom would brighten her wardrobe. Dan's gift was a long cushion for the seat of her wooden bench and matching pads for the back.

"I noticed you needed these when I visited," he smiled. "That 'sofa' wasn't the best for comfort."

"Thank you! Thank you all!" she exclaimed wiping away happy tears.

Though Christmas Eve had been the crowning event, the following days were filled with much warm family enjoyment. Dan spent Christmas Day with them and the afternoon was filled with more delicious food, games, and snacking. Hot cups of chocolate "Famoso de Abuelita" (Grandma's Famous) heaped with whipped cream were the final hit of the day.

At last, things settled back to daily ranch life. Nancy spent several hours with Dad taking feed to the cattle, helping fix a damaged gate. She loved the time to hear his farm news and to share her stories from across the border with him.

She and Mom had so many wonderful chats as they worked together or just sat basking in one another's company. Each evening Nancy whispered her prayer of gratitude. "Jesus, thank you, thank you for these precious days."

She shared with her parents the dream of having Joey visit her a few days during his spring break. They agreed it would be an unforgettable experience for him. The decision was made to plan for his trip.

One morning she and Joey saddled Champ and Goldie for a brisk ride across the ranch. They soon slowed their horses to a moderate gait and began to reminisce.

"Remember the time," Joey began, "when I insisted on wading in the pond and I slipped and fell in the muddy bottom. What a sight I was! I didn't want Mom to see me like that. So, you rinsed me off at the pump. Man! Was I cold! That water made icicles on my elbows!"

Nancy laughed, "And do you remember the time we tried to help the newborn calf back from the pasture. The mama cow didn't exactly like our ideas. We decided Mama knew best and left them to manage on their own, which they did very well."

On they went with one tale after another of growing up years accompanied by gales of laughter and some sobering thoughts as well.

And so, passed too quickly the wondrous week. One more of Mom's culinary successes finalized the visit after church on Sunday. It was decided that Dad and Joey would take Nancy to her bus while Dan stayed to help Mom with cleanup and dish washing.

Goodbyes were said with several reminders that the months would pass quickly. Joey was elated with prospects of his visit to Puesta del Sol during spring vacation.

"We'll phone often," Mom called as Dad's truck began to move and then hurried to soothe the departure pain in the awaiting kitchen duties.

"You should visit her in the village," Dan urged as they began to collect dishes from the table.

"I'd surely like to," Mom agreed.

"You'd truly enjoy getting acquainted with Myra next door and with all those village folks. Being there makes you see how much she is loved and accepted. They would do anything for Miss Nancy."

"You're convincing me," Mom smiled. "Maybe I can just do that."

Kitchen work finished, Dan paused at the door.

"Mom Jefferson, I wish you'd pray for me." He paused. "Sometimes I feel like I should be involved in mission work doing something like Nancy is. I could see the need when I was there."

"I will pray, Dan, I surely will and God will show you His plan."

Chapter 11

The Rains, The Kitten, and The Monster

Nancy started up the hill which seemed longer than usual today. The rain-soaked earth had become slippery and clinging. Every time she took a step her shoes picked up another layer of the sticky clay.

"I'll be two inches taller by the time I get to Laura's door," Nancy half chuckled.

She plodded on, catching her breath when her feet almost went out from under her. Quite breathless, she reached the top of the incline and crossed Laura's patio. Feelings both of anticipation and dread struggled to dominate her thoughts as she neared the kitchen door. Would Grandma

Victoria be her old vibrant self or would she still be down with that nagging fatigue?

Nancy kicked off her muddy shoes and tapped at the door. Grandma responded from inside and Nancy entered to find her elderly friend seated at the table picking over beans for supper.

"Ay, Mi Hijita! You're back! How we missed you!"

"How are you, Grandma?"

"Oh, I'm fine!" Grandma smiled her best. "Now that you're here."

Laura stepped in from the adjoining room. After warm greetings and questions about Nancy's vacation and home folks, Laura turned her attention to the beans Grandma had picked over.

"It's enough for supper, isn't it?" Grandma questioned.

"That's plenty," Laura agreed.

"I guess I'll rest just a little bit then."

With a hug for Nancy, Grandma disappeared behind the bedroom curtain. A look of concern crossed Nancy's face as she turned to Laura.

"She's still very tired, isn't she? Do you think she'd like me to take her into San Diego to Doctor Canales?"

"We'd be so relieved if we could know what's wrong and get some help," Laura sighed. "It would be almost impossible to take her on the bus."

"I know," Nancy agreed. "Could you go along tomorrow?"

"I'm sure I can. I'll talk it over with Grandma when she gets up."

"She was a little hard to convince," Laura confided as she and Nancy settled into Dr. Canales' waiting room chairs, next afternoon.

Their wait was brief as Grandma appeared quite soon through the door of the doctor's consulting room. She was wearing a smile nearly too wide for her petite face to contain.

Merrily shaking a small bottle of pills above her head she announced, "Iron pills to build up my blood! Doctor says I'll be as spry as a kid goat in no time."

The ride home was one of celebration and blessed relief over the doctor's diagnosis.

A good night's sleep brought Nancy expectantly to her front door next morning. Could it be that this constant rain was coming to an end?

"Dear Lord," she breathed. "How I'd love to see one tangerine dawn!"

Her gaze drifted to the path leading from the street to the very door where her eyes focused on a huge fuzzy black spider advancing toward the now inviting entrance.

Nancy's cry of dismay reached Myra's back patio where this unsuspecting lady was tidying up in the early morning light. Dropping her broom, she scurried toward the fence which separated the two houses.

In the meantime, Nancy's leap of Olympic proportions had landed her safely behind a frantically slammed door.

"Na-a-a-ancy," came the elongated call. "What's going on over there?"

Myra's thoroughly shaken neighbor crept to crack open her window and peered next door.

"Oh, Myra!" Nancy shuddered. "There is the awfulest, ugliest creature crawling up my walk! He is monstrous and he was headed right for my door! Myra, what am I going to do?"

"Hang on, Nancy. I'll send Enrique right over."

"Tell him to be careful."

"Do you think he should take his rifle?" Myra was chuckling now.

"Oh Myra, you're making fun of me!" Nancy

scolded.

"I'm sorry, dear friend!" After a suppressed giggle, Myra went on more sympathetically. "I know this is your first tarantula and they are ugly! They tend to come out of their holes when it rains like this. Enrique will get rid of him right away for you. He's on his way."

Nancy covered her ears at the sound of two powerful blows just outside her door. A knock followed.

Enrique stood there with the immobilized creature on the blade of his machete.

"Is he dead?" Nancy queried.

"Quite dead," Enrique smiled. "But I'd advise you to be careful. These fellows probably won't hurt anyone unless they're cornered."

"But you killed him, Enrique," Nancy shivered.

"He just might have a wife and children," Enrique returned quizzically.

"Enrique!" Nancy shrieked.

His voice softened. "Sorry! I didn't say that just to scare you. I just want you to be cautious. It would really be safer to put muddy boots inside. They could give one of these beasts a cozy place to crawl into. And he might object to your fitting your toes in beside him."

"They-they would do that?" Nancy gasped.

"It's possible," he replied. "Just be careful and call us anytime you need anything. We're right next door, you know!"

"Thank you! Thank you! Good neighbor."

He smiled and waved as he picked up his machete and the remains of the dreadful creature which minutes before had been threatening Nancy's security.

Scratch-scratch-scratch. Nancy stirred. She'd been dreaming that an immense tarantula was crawling into one of her muddy boots. Scratch-scratch. Could that awful thing or one of his relatives be threatening revenge? She was out of bed in an instant ready to call Enrique for the second time.

She peered through the front window; no sign of a menacing furry spider. Instead, her gaze fell on a tiny ball of gray fur looking out of pleading emerald eyes.

"Oh! You precious baby!" Nancy cried as she flung wide the door and scooped up the fluffy mite. The kitten nestled against Nancy's chin and with the muted rumble in its tiny throat, began its song of praise.

Nancy placed a towel over Dan's gift of the

sofa mat. Lifting the little stray, she laid her there as she hurried to the kitchen for a saucer of warm milk.

"Well, I guess you smelled breakfast, didn't you?" Nancy laughed.

The little stranger lapped voraciously then sat by the empty saucer, bright eyes fixed on its rescuer.

"Are you still hungry? Well, just a little more. Then we're going to see Myra."

"What in the world do you have there?" Myra demanded as Nancy entered her kitchen. Nancy turned the little animal toward her neighbor.

"It was scratching at my door just now. Do you think it belongs to someone?"

"I have no idea. Maybe nobody was caring for it since it wandered to your doorway. But we can ask around."

"It's such a darling. I'd love to keep it, but if it belongs to someone…" Nancy trailed off.
"Don't worry! It probably needs a good home."

"It should have a name just in case no one claims it. What could we call it?" Nancy questioned.

"Why, Huerfanita," came Myra's quick reply.

"Huerfanita? I guess that's a new word for me," Nancy came back.

"It's a child who has lost his parents and been left alone," Myra translated.

"Oh, of course–Little Orphan," Nancy processed under her breath.

Then aloud, "Perfect! But I don't know if it's a boy or girl."

"Has to be a girl with those dazzling eyes and silky fur," Myra deducted. "But just in case it turns out to be a boy, you can switch to 'Huerfanito.'"

"Simple!" Nancy agreed.

"One thing you must remember," Myra went on, a bit of mischief in her eyes.

"Huerfanita is a Mexican cat, you know. She won't come if you call her 'Kee-ty, Kee-ty, Kee-ty' like you Americans do. You must call 'Sh, Sh, Sh'. Then she'll be at your feet in an instant."

Huerfanita's little head turned immediately toward Myra at the familiar call.

"See, she knows already," Myra announced.

"I guess you've proved your point." Nancy joined in Myra's laughter.

Huerfanita made herself right at home. In fact, as Nancy awoke next morning, she found the kitten cozily curled up on her pillow.

"Why you little rascal!" Nancy scolded. "Who told you that you could share my bed?" But she didn't push the small intruder off on the floor.

"I think the Lord sent you to cheer me up during these dreary days. Just hear that downpour out there!" she continued the one-sided conversation with the tiny feline.

"Which reminds me. You drank most of the milk yesterday. Before we can have breakfast, I'm going to have to trudge down the street for a panful. Chela will have the goats milked by the time I get there."

She couldn't resist picking Huerfanita up to stroke her soft fur. Nancy replaced the kitten on the warm pillow and quickly dressed. With jacket, rain hood and boots, she braved the dreaded rain. It had fortunately let up to a drizzle. Her path led down past the once dry creek bed.

This morning, brown water hissed and spun angrily through the widening channel the deluge was forming. The scene Nancy encountered as she turned toward the little goat ranch at village end stopped her in her tracks. Big Don Tomas, his face a mask of anguish, came rushing toward her, the body of his small son clutched to his breast. A crowd of panicked villagers followed at his heels.

"Miss Nancy! Miss Nancy! He slipped into

the water! He's not breathing! Help me!" The big man's voice broke.

By now, Nancy was on her knees, her discarded jacket on the ground before her.

"Place him here," she instructed. Immediately assuming the professional calm of a nurse in charge, she attempted to reassure the distraught crowd. She felt none of that needed calm within her own quaking heart.

Desperately, she cried to the Heavenly Father as she positioned the little boy's body and methodically, purposefully began the process of resuscitation.

With each movement, a silent prayer went up. "Jesus help me! Please, please, restore this little life!"

Muffled sobs came from the breathless crowd. An arm was thrown around Don Tomas. The rain continued.

Nancy felt a light blanket placed around her shoulders. She labored on.

"Jesus, please!" she pleaded.

And then the desperately hoped-for gasp from the child… He drew in air! He was breathing!

Sobs of relief! Cries of joy from those who had suffered through this terrible ordeal… Don Tomas on his knees beside his son, tears streaming down his weathered face.

"Keep him warm," Nancy cautioned as the man lifted his precious boy into his arms again.

"Oh, Miss Nancy!" he sobbed. "What if you hadn't been here! What if you hadn't been here!"

"I'm so thankful I was! God knew!" she responded, her voice breaking from the tension and relief.

"I'll check on him this afternoon."

Slowly the crowd dispersed. Wearily, she retraced her steps to her own door.

Huerfanita met her with a forlorn accusing look in those emerald eyes.

"Where have you been!" she seemed to demand. "Didn't you plan to bring me back some milk!"

"You poor little thing!" Nancy soothed. "Let's make some oatmeal to add to that bit of milk."

With an impatient flick of the tail, Huerfanita marched toward the kitchen giving one quick glance back to see that her neglectful provider was following. Minutes later the irate kitten was happily lapping up her new tasty treat. Nancy sank into a chair. Huerfanita soon leaped into her lap.

"If you only knew, Little One! If you only knew. God has done a miracle, putting me right in the path of a terrible disaster, at the very moment I was needed. I'm so thankful! So thankful I was there!"

Again, there echoed in her thoughts Don Tomas' tearful exclamation, "What if you hadn't been here!"

Shortly after lunch, Nancy gathered her stethoscope and a few small treats for Don Tomas' children. She trudged the few blocks to his home.

Dona Lita met Nancy at the door, tears in her eyes.

"Miss Nancy! Miss Nancy! You saved our boy! Thank you! Thank you!"

"It is God we truly have to thank, dear lady," Nancy responded softly.

Don Tomas joined Nancy and his wife. "Yes, we do know it was God's great mercy for our Tomasito. The poor little guy tripped and that slippery bank sent him sliding into the water. I ran! How I ran… desperate to catch him but the water was so swift! In God's mercy his clothes caught on the branch that hangs over the creek bed farther down. I could reach him. And then you were right there! God was so good to us."

Nancy knelt to check the little boy's chest. She could find no problem as she listened to his lungs.

His adoring older sisters were showering him with rapt attention. In turn, they were bringing some of their own treasures to entertain him as he sat on the floor in their midst. Nancy smiled at the scene.

"Tomasito, here is my book you always like to look at."

Nancy placed her treats in the hand of one of the little girls.

"Oh look! Tomasito. Look what Miss Nancy brought us! You can choose first what you like best."

"I believe everything is OK," Nancy advised the parents. "Call for me anytime you have a concern."

"Thank you, Miss Nancy. We can't thank you enough," Lita whispered.

And just as she was ready to leave the little house, Don Tomas added,

"We'll be in church Sunday. God has been so merciful. We need to be in His house on His day."

It was with a much lighter step that Nancy made her way homeward. Once in her own living room, tremendous feelings of relief, as well as emotional and physical exhaustion engulfed her.

"Jesus," she whispered as her head rested on a welcoming pillow. "Could you please arrange a tangerine sunset soon!" Huerfanita snuggled beside her and they slept.

Sometime later a soft tapping at her door aroused Nancy. Myra stood outside with a concerned look on her face.

"It's been so quiet over here all afternoon. I wondered if you were all right."

"Oh, yes," Nancy responded, "after a good nap. Thank you, friend."

"You had quite a morning. If you feel like talking, we would like you to join us for supper. It will be ready in a bit."

Nancy sighed with the anticipation of warm food and the thoughtful couple's company.

"That will do me so much good," she smiled. "I'll be there."

At her neighbor's kitchen door, the essence of friendship, understanding, and love engulfed Nancy with the warmth of Myra's fire.

Conversation over her hostess' refried beans and enchiladas further undid the clinging tensions of the frightful morning. "Thank you, dear friends," Nancy breathed gratefully as she prepared to leave.

"Oh Nancy!" Myra's look stopped her at the door. "God had you there this morning! What if it hadn't been that way? Be thankful! Be comforted! It was His marvelous plan!"

Sunday morning, true to his word, Don Tomas sat proudly at one end of a church bench with Dona Lita at the other. Between their parents, whispering excitedly, sat the four young Garzas. Nancy's heart swelled as she rose to give the opening story. Her animated account was especially directed to the children but enjoyed by all. A little boy's life had been saved. Now a whole family sat listening to the life-giving Word of God. How eternally grateful she would be.

Nancy desperately hoped for a change in the weather as a new week began but the stubborn clouds remained with alternating downpours and chilling mist. Ever since she had returned from her wondrous Christmas break, this lovely Puesta del Sol had become a sodden huddle of adobe homes. The village crouched against the once protective ranges which now only funneled unwanted moisture into the muddy streets.

Sunday church folks slugged through the wet, leaving their mud-caked shoes on the doorstep. Nancy wondered if the pile of footwear could ever be sorted out for the waiting shivery feet of those valiant church goers. Where in the world would there be such another faithful flock?

The gloomy days passed one by one. Friday morning Nancy caught her breath as she peered through the front door. A small patch of blue sky greeted her hopeful gaze. She lingered in the patio among her plants, stirring the water soaked soil around their roots.

"Poor things," she whispered. "You need to breathe."

Before turning indoors, Nancy cast another wistful glance skyward. It did seem that the beautiful blue rift in the clouds was the tiniest bit larger.

Sunday's preparations and other duties kept her occupied until late afternoon though her eyes wandered often to her west window. Surely her yearning prayers were being answered. As she cleared supper dishes from the table shafts of brilliant sun suddenly lit her living room.

She flew to the front door. Scurrying dark clouds were now tinted with purple. Orange rays filled the vault above.

"Myra! Myra!" Nancy shrilled. "Come see what God is doing!"

"Oh Nancy!" Myra breathed as she joined her neighbor.

They stood together, silenced by the glorious display. Then, Myra burst into the doxology. Nancy joined in. They sang in joyful worship. Then, they sang it again softly, slowly savoring the words.

Chapter 12
Ofelia and Restoration

Laura lifted her eyes from her morning coffee as Otoniel's shadow darkened the kitchen door.

"I didn't hear you get up and leave."

"You were worn out with all you've been doing over at Ofelia's these days."

"Did you go over there?"

He nodded.

"And?"

"No baby yet!" He slumped beside her at the table.

"Laura, I can't stand to see my little sister suffer so...all day yesterday and all night last night!"

"What does Genoveva say, Otoniel? She has handled birthings all over this village for years."

"She's doing all she knows to help Ofelia. She was with her all night."

He shook his head. "I'm scared, Laura. Women have died in childbirth. What are we going to do?"

She laid her hand on his arm. "Otoniel, there's Nancy."

He remained silent.

"Otoniel?"

"How can we go to her? I've ignored her, avoided her, and refused to let the kids go there."

"Maybe this is the time to make things right," she responded.

"Maybe," he whispered.

Getting up, he paced around the table.

"I can't!" he burst out.

"Yes, you can. We have to. Nancy is not a person who holds a grudge. She'll help us. She will!"

"Then you'll go with me?"

"Yes, of course I will."

Nancy answered her door, rather surprised to find both Laura and Otoniel standing outside. She held out a hand to each of them.

"Come in!" she invited.

"Otoniel has something to tell you," Laura began.

He hesitated… then, "Miss Nancy, we're in trouble. I don't deserve your help after the way I've treated you. I wouldn't have come except…" he fought for control.

"Miss Nancy, my little sister hasn't been able to give birth. She's suffering so! Could you check on her to see what's wrong?" the man shuddered.

"Please forgive me for my inexcusable attitude and for shutting you out of our lives."

"Of course, I do, Otoniel. I understand. I do." She held out her hand. He grasped it.

"Thank you, Miss Nancy! Thank you so much!"

"I'm not a doctor you know," she cautioned. "But I'll do anything I can to help. Maybe we need to take her into the hospital in San Diego. I can go to see her with you now, if you like."

"Please!" Otoniel breathed.

Laura and Otoniel stood outside the bedroom door as Nancy checked the young expectant mother. She questioned Genoveva and then Ofelia as she went through a process of trying to pinpoint possible problems.

She faced the worried couple just outside. "I think it would be best to take her into the hospital," she told them softly.

"I think she's ready for some answers," Nancy added. "If you want to talk with her husband and get her prepared to go, I'll bring the car up here."

"I'll tell Jaime," Otoniel nodded. "He's pretty worried."

With a blanket and pillow arranged on the passenger seat so Ofelia could be as comfortable as possible, they were quickly on their way.

Laura murmured reassurance from the back seat.

Each moan from their passenger served to increase Nancy's pressure on the gas pedal. Just as they entered San Diego's city limits she heard the scream of a siren.

"Oh, no!" she groaned.

Slowing to a stop she faced the young officer whose motorcycle screeched to a halt beside her window. He was already writing a ticket.

"You speak Spanish?" he questioned.

"Yes, Sir," she answered meekly.

"You were speeding," he accused.

"I know, Sir, but this young lady is about to give birth. We have to get her to the hospital!"

The man cast one glance at Ofelia's tortured form.

"Follow me!" he thundered.

The roar of his bike exploded in the quiet street as he raced ahead with Nancy in hot pursuit.

In minutes they had pulled into the Emergency Entrance of San Diego's Community Hospital. The officer was at the door calling for help. Almost immediately a stalwart attendant was standing at the car window sizing up the situation.

"How much do you weigh?" he was questioning Ofelia.

She could only shake her head before he had opened the car door and picked her up bodily. The police officer seemed to react as if this were routine.

He held the emergency door wide for this unceremonious entrance to the hospital. Both Nancy and Laura, taken aback by the proceedings, tried to express their profuse gratitude to their guide.

"My job," he winked as he tore a speeding ticket in half.

"You'd better get in there with your friend." He stepped toward his cycle.

"Thank you and goodbye!" The ladies called after him. He lifted his hand in a farewell salute.

Inside they settled into seats in a nearly empty waiting area. They waited…The wall clock ticked.

Minutes seemed to linger agonizingly over every tick while the ladies fidgeted.

Laura glanced up at that aggravating timepiece. "Have we only been here fifteen minutes? It seems like an hour at least!"

"Let's pray," Nancy suggested. Grasping one another's hands, they bowed in earnest supplication for Ofelia's safe delivery of a healthy baby.

The afternoon dragged on. They were becoming exhausted with the stress of the long wait, when the intercom finally clicked to life. "Hernan Ortiz" it announced. "Critical." "Emilia Lopez-Released." Patient after patient was named along with his or her terse medical evaluation in one of three categories: "Critical", "Delicate", or "Released".

They strained for word of Ofelia. Then it came. "Ofelia Garza: Delicate".

Laura clutched Nancy's arm. "She must have had the baby."

"Let's ask if they'll permit us to see her," from Nancy.

"Right this way," a smiling young nurse directed.

Ofelia greeted them with a weak, but joyful smile as she cuddled her newborn.

"Come meet my little son!"

"Oh, how precious!" Nancy exclaimed.

Laura bent to peer at her newest nephew. Curling lashes brushed pink cheeks as the infant squinted against the light of this intruding world. But the half smile on the tiny lips seemed to say, "I'm glad I'm here."

"Ofelia, he's beautiful!" Laura spoke with tears in her adoring brown eyes. "We're so thankful! We just waited and prayed out there."

"And God helped me so much! Thank you, Laura and thank you, Miss Nancy! Thank you! Thank you!"

"We'll take the good news back to the village now and be here for you when you're released," Nancy reassured the new mother.

Ofelia squeezed Nancy's hand. "Tomorrow about this time," she whispered sleepily. "Thank you, dear girls."

As Nancy's blue Volkswagen turned into Puesta del Sol's narrow streets, the whole village seemed to pour from doorways. Sisters, aunts, cousins, neighbors crowded to the car windows.

"How is Ofelia?"

"Did she have the baby?"

"Boy or girl?"

"Did you see her? The baby?"

Jaime came running from his corral. A few of the crowded villagers parted to allow him to reach the car.

The look on Nancy's and Laura's faces told him all was well.

"She's all right!" he sobbed.

"Yes, and you have a beautiful son," Laura smiled.

With tears running down his cheeks, the strain of these terrible hours drained from his being. He lifted his hand to the Giver of all good gifts.

"My wife is all right! And I have a little boy! Thank God! Thank God!"

Chapter 13
What If?

The new mother was home. Nancy let the weekend pass wanting to give Jaime and Ofelia some space with their tiny son. She knew that Grandma and Laura were eagerly available for the little family's every need.

There were preparations for the Sunday's service as well as Monday children's time which kept her occupied on Saturday. Sunday morning Nancy thrilled with thanksgiving at the sight of a few new faces in the service; among them Otoniel, Laura and their three little ones. Several greeted her, mentioning their gratitude for her part in Ofelia's joyous event.

A lady Nancy had not seen before confided

earnestly, "How grateful we are that you were here. I don't know what we'd have done without you."

"Jaime's mother," Myra whispered as the woman moved on.

"Oh!" Nancy breathed a quick "Thank you, Lord." How often she and Myra prayed together for more of the villagers to hear the message of Jesus' great love and to experience the gift of a changed life. She almost burst with happiness Monday afternoon as she opened the door to Jose Luis, Josefina and Clarisa! What a change in Otoniel! To think he'd been in church yesterday with his family. Now he was permitting the children to come to Bible story time. The others soon arrived and they began their singing.

As Nancy started today's story of Jesus and the lepers, she had to clear her throat frequently. At last, she paused and apologized to the children.

"I guess I have a frog in my throat," she explained.

She was unprepared for their sudden burst into gales of laughter. Puzzled, she waited for the merriment to subside a bit.

"I didn't know that was so funny," she smiled.

This provoked more giggling.

"Can you tell me why you are so amused this afternoon?" Nancy was finally able to ask between their fits of laughter and efforts to show respect for their teacher.

"Oh, Miss Nancy, we don't say we have a 'frog' in our throats." More giggles.

"Miss Nancy, when we have to go 'ahem, ahem' we have a 'chicken' in our throats."

Then it was Nancy's turn to laugh.

"A chicken!" she exclaimed. "Then I must take out the frog and put in a chicken."

"Yes! Yes!" they chorused amid clapping and settling back to enjoy the remainder of Nancy's Bible story.

At the close of Bible time, Nancy decided to accompany Laura and Otoniel's three up the hill for a visit and some news of Ofelia's baby. She found Grandma finishing the hem in a tiny nightgown.

"Oh, they are just fine," she chuckled at Nancy's inquiry. Pride over her newest grandson shone all over Grandma's face.

"They brought the little one over here so I could see him. These old legs just don't want to carry me that far. Ofelia wants to see you, Miss Nancy. When you leave, maybe you could trot over there and," she paused, "carry this nightie along?"

"Of course, I will, Grandma."

After a few minutes of chatting and a good laugh over the tale of the frog and the chicken, Nancy was on her way toward Jaime's and Ofelia's small home.

"Sit right here, Miss Nancy," Ofelia invited as she drew a bench away from the table. "I want you to hold the baby."

"Oh, I'd love to," Nancy responded. "What did you name him?" she wanted to know as she gazed captivated by the tiny nose and petite puckered lips.

"I was hoping you'd ask because, if you didn't, I was going to tell you."

Ofelia's eyes sparkled. "We are calling him 'Nathanael,'" she announced.

"And this is why... because the name ends like Otoniel who brought you to us and because," she paused, "because it begins like Nancy.

Miss Nancy, you can't imagine how thankful Jaime and I are for what you did for me. I don't know what would have happened if you hadn't been here. You aren't going to leave us, are you, Miss Nancy?"

Nancy mulled over Ofelia's plea as she started

slowly toward home. Don Tomas had said it. Dona Lita had echoed his words. Myra had voiced her concerns that Nancy's year was passing so quickly. And yesterday, it was Jaime's mother. Could it be, that in God's plan, this was not to be a one year assignment? What did God want? What might this mean?

Chapter 14
Joey

Nancy awoke with the delicious sense that something very special was to take place today.

Joey! Yes, he'd be in Puesta del Sol within hours!

She bounced from bed. What first? Her prayer time, of course. Earnestly, she lifted her little brother to the Lord. She prayed for this adventure for him, that would be all for good, that he would fit in with the village boys, and the language would not be a barrier, that Joey would find these young villagers to be very much like his friends at home, accepting, fun-loving, just boys like himself.

She rose from her knees reassured and anxious to finish preparations for his arrival. Now what needed to be done? The spaghetti and meatballs, his favorite, were ready in the refrigerator. She'd stir up the peanut butter cookies after a quick breakfast.

Cookies baked and put away, Nancy checked the clock. Still three hours before she could plan on that bus coming in with Joey aboard. She glanced around. Joey's cot bed was made up in the corner of the living room. He could have a little privacy behind the screen she had fashioned.

A tap at the door caught her attention.

"Come," she called and Myra peeped in.

"Are you still busy?" her neighbor greeted.

"No!" Nancy responded. "And I'm so excited and so bored all at once!"

"Come over and have a couple tacos with me." Myra went on. "Enrique had a trip into San Diego this morning and I'm lonesome. I've got refries."

"I'm with you!" from Nancy. How she relished those mashed beans lightly fried and spread on a warm tortilla.

They crossed Myra's patio and into her kitchen where lunch smells reminded Nancy that she was hungry.

"Oh Myra! You always come to my rescue! I didn't know what to do with myself after everything was ready."

"Let's eat. Then we can have a prayer for Joey and his time here. I can hardly wait to meet him! I know he's going to love being with you and with all of us!"

And so, with Myra's spritely company that slow-ticking clock seemed to speed up and it was nearing bus time.

"You go by yourself so he won't be overpowered by a welcoming committee," Myra suggested.

"Alright, but I know he'll want to meet you right away. I've told him so much about my neighbors."

"See you then," Myra waved.

Joey was the first one down the steps as the driver opened the bus door.

"Buenos dias!" he greeted his big sister. Nancy laughed and threw her arms around the boy she'd so lovingly waited for.

"Very good! But since it is afternoon you could say 'Buenas tardes.'"

"Oh...so 'dias' is for morning and 'tardes' is for afternoon. What's for night?"

"Buenas noches', but let's drop the Spanish lesson for now.

Tell me about your trip and about everybody

at home. Oh! I've got so many questions!"

And so, the pleasant chatter went on as they slowly covered the distance to Nancy's little house.

"This is where you live?" Joey questioned.

"Come on in. You'll love it."

"Cool!" was Joey's verdict as he surveyed the neat little kitchen and the living room with his arranged sleeping area.

"Are you hungry?" Nancy queried as they set down her brother's luggage.

"Sure!" came Joey's rather expected answer. "I'm always hungry!"

"How about some peanut butter cookies and milk?"

"Terrific!" Joey slid into the kitchen chair and put his elbows on the table.

Nancy didn't correct him as she placed the goodies within his reach.

"What's for supper?"

"You are hungry!" Nancy laughed. "I have spaghetti and meatballs in the refrigerator."

"Really? Wow! Though I was hoping for pinto beans and jalapenos."

"And you shall have them," Nancy promised.

"They are yummy—only for me, light on the jalapenos."

"Are you up to meeting my good neighbors or do you just want to relax a while?" Nancy asked, conscious that this boy had had a long day already.

"Enrique and Myra? Let's go!"

Across the way Myra held out welcoming arms as they entered her patio.

"We're oh so happy you're here," she beamed.

Nancy translated.

The sound of Enrique's truck pulling to a stop caught their attention. The good-natured driver was out of the vehicle in a moment.

"Joey!" he boomed extending a friendly hand.

Joey grasped the offered hand while hurriedly rehearsing Nancy's instructions for the proper greeting.

"Buenas tardes," he responded proudly.

After a most successful spaghetti and meatball supper, Nancy left the dishes. She so wanted to catch up on all the news of home. Joey chatted on and on while Huerfanita purred in his lap.

"You know I think this has been a kinda long day," he wound down at last. "Guess I'll try that cot over there. I'm going to help you with the dishes first."

Nancy remonstrated, but Joey insisted. So, they enjoyed a few more minutes of happy chatter while Nancy washed and Joey dried and stacked dishes.

Dishes done, Nancy busied herself with getting Joey's bedtime pan of warm water while he returned to the living room.

"Oh! Oh!" She heard his amused exclamation. "Looks like I've got company."

Nancy peered around the kitchen door. Having lost her place on Joey's lap, Huerfanita was now curled up on his cot.

"Huerfanita!" Nancy scolded as she scooped up the unsuspecting trespasser. "This is not your bed!" Shaking her finger at the little opportunist, she continued to lay down the law.

Joey watched grinning at the whole procedure.

"I think you're getting through to her," he teased. "But don't worry. She's welcome in my bedroom."

"Well, alright, Joey, but let me know if she bothers. Sleep well! Good night, little brother."

"Good night, big sis."

They had scarcely finished breakfast and a prayer time next morning when shouts from the street called them to the window.

Five boys stood outside the patio wall waving a soccer ball.

"Joey! Joey! Joey!" came their singsong shout.

"They want you to play soccer with them," Nancy laughed.

"Shall I go?"

"Of course, if you like," she urged.

"Buenos dias!" Joey shouted as he trotted down the patio path.

"Buenos dias," they chorused laughing.

Pointing to himself, he repeated his name. He then pointed to the first boy in the street line-up.

"Beto," the boy responded.

"Beto," Joey repeated. He pointed to the next soccer player.

"Rolando," the boy answered.

"Ro-lan-do," Joey pronounced carefully.

And so on down the line through "Juan", "Javier" and "Noberto".

This process of introductions complete, a shout of "Vamanos!" (Let's go!) rose from several lips.

"Vamanos!" Joey echoed.

Laughing and racing down the street, the group arrived at the playing field and the game began.

So went the week with a game nearly every day. Joey was shouting "cabeza" (head) as loudly and frequently as the others. He would arrive at Nancy's door perspiring and dirt-smudged.

After his clean-up, Joey would spend the rest of the day "at your service, Nancy". He washed her car, swept the back patio, and helped her move some heavy plant pots to more sunny areas. After the Sunday service in Puesta del Sol, they took a picnic. Shade was scanty among the cacti and palms on the way to La Mesa but they did find a cool spot to eat their egg sandwiches, cookies, and fruit.

"So, the man we'll meet was your Spanish teacher."

"Yes, Joey, and a good one. He's teaching the village children now. You must see his classroom and meet his sweet mom."

Though he didn't understand much of the conversation, Joey marveled as Miguel showed him his meagerly furnished classroom, his few textbooks and homemade charts.

Miguel's mother called them for sweet rolls and hot chocolate before they left.

"Wow, Nance!" Joey exclaimed as they headed back across the stream between the two villages.

"He's a great guy, isn't he? Imagine him teaching all those grades with so few books and supplies!

"He's preparing them to go into town to continue their studies. He's doing his best," Nancy responded.

Nancy's Monday Bible hour began with quite a noisy clamor.

"Joey! Joey!" came a shout from one young hopeful. "Sit here beside me!"

"No! No! Joey!" from another direction. "I saved a place here for you!"

"Joey!" "Joey!" "Joey!" "Here!" "Here!" the competition continued.

Nancy hushed her children and solved the problem by dividing them into small groups with Joey assigned to each during a specific activity.

"What's next?" Joey wanted to know as the last children said goodbye, waving at the door.

"Shall we visit Grandma Victoria tomorrow?"

"Yes! Yes! I can hardly wait to meet her. How do I say 'Grandma' in Spanish?" Joey asked as they began to climb to her door next afternoon.

"Abuela," Nancy supplied.

"A-bue-la," he repeated. "What else can I say?"

"It would please her immensely if you would say 'Te quiero, Abuela.'" (I love you, Grandma.)

Joey repeated the phrase.

They found Grandma Victoria seated on her bench near the kitchen stove.

"Joey!" she grinned. "You came to see me!"

"Buenas tardes, Abuela."

"Oh, Nancy!" Grandma was chuckling in pure joy at this greeting from Nancy's little brother.

"I knew you would have the most handsome brother and he speaks Spanish!"

Grandma patted the end of her bench, inviting Joey to sit down. He promptly accepted at which Grandma placed a wrinkled hand on each of Joey's cheeks.

He glanced at Nancy. She nodded.

"Te quiero, Abuela." he said. Grandma beamed.

With Nancy as interpreter, the minutes flew. At last she glanced at her watch and knew they must bring the delightful visit to a close.

"You come see me again," Grandma invited.

"Next time, Grandma," Joey returned.

"La proxima vez," Nancy prompted.

Joey repeated the Spanish words. Grandma

clapped her hands but no one could guess that there would be no "next time". On they went, spending a few minutes with Ofelia and baby Nathanael now a chubby, chuckling darling.

Once again on the village street, Joey questioned, "Is this the lady you rushed to the hospital so that little guy could be born?"

Nancy nodded.

"And you almost got a speeding ticket," he grinned. "Wow Nance! No wonder you love it here. Everything is an adventure."

"An adventure with the Lord, Joey."

"I know. I think the Lord must have an adventure for me, too. I'm praying about it."

"He does have and He will lead you to it. He surely will!"

"Just like he did you, right?"

"Absolutely!"

Their visiting ended with a stop to see Tomasito and family. Joey had been the one to get Nancy's call home after the little boy's near drowning. Now he was to meet the child he had prayed for.

Joey was silent as they turned again toward Nancy's adobe home.

"Your thoughts?" Nancy asked.

"God does miracles, doesn't He, Nance? That little guy is one of them."

"Yes, Joey. I know God was in every single step we took that day and Tomasito was saved."

Over supper, Nancy suggested a trip into San Diego for Wednesday.

"Great!" was Joey's response.

She recounted the story of Miguel Hidalgo as they rode toward town quite early in the morning. She tried to paint a picture of the Independence Day celebration they had attended her first days in Puesta del Sol.

"After about ten years of struggle they finally won their independence from Spain," Nancy concluded.

She drove by the town plaza to point out the balcony from which Mayor Cardenas had shouted "Viva Mexico!" She described the festive celebrating crowd and their roar of response.

"Wish I'd been here," Joey enthused.

"Maybe another time," Nancy replied.

He looked at her quizzically. "Another time?" Wasn't she coming home to stay this fall? Since she said no more, he didn't press the question.

Joey whistled his surprise when they pulled into San Diego's Supermarket.

"This isn't much different from home!"

"It really isn't, is it?" Nancy smiled. "Just like shopping at Johnson's Grocery in Midland."

With a stop for tacos and Joey's jalapenos, there was only one thing left to do; a visit to the confectionery for a frosty trolley bus.

"This really makes my day!" Joey smiled. "Thank you, Nance. Thank you."

Their successful day complete, Nancy turned the blue VW back toward the village.

Hours flew by as Joey's vacation days were winding down—one more soccer game, more sister-brother chats.

Myra insisted on a "goodbye lunch" before Joey's bus time.

"I'm going to miss your cooking," he advised her as he gobbled seconds of capirotada (her tasty dessert).

They shared big hugs at the door. Joey thanked them again and again for all they had done to make his vacation "a winner".

He added, "And for being such great neighbors to my big sister."

"You keep studying that Spanish," Enrique challenged. "Next time, you and I are going to swap stories."

Nancy and Joey wandered slowly up to the bus stop where Joey would soon board and begin his trip homeward. A dust cloud announced the approach of the unwelcome vehicle. Tears threatened as Nancy watched Joey climb aboard. He lingered on the bus step.

"Adiós!" he shouted. "Te quiero."

"Love you, too."

She waved as long as the lumbering bus was in sight.

Chapter 15
Heavenward

Nancy trudged slowly up the slope toward Laura's patio. She was apprehensive about what she would find behind her neighbor's kitchen door. Grandma Victoria just wasn't doing well. Slowly but surely, she was losing her usual strength and sparkle. They had taken her back to Dr. Canales. He wasn't able to give them much encouragement.

"I think it's her age," he had confided to Laura as Nancy guided Grandma through the waiting room and toward her car.

"Organs tend to weaken and it's hard to arrest that process. I can give you a prescription that may help for awhile."

Grandma had taken her pills rather disinterestedly and had asked Otoniel to move her small cot next to the kitchen stove. Though spring sunshine was warming the days, Grandma always seemed to need the warmth of the fire.

Today, as Nancy opened the door, Grandma's face lit up. She welcomed her visitor from her cozy place by the stove.

"Oh, Mi Hijita!" (my daughter or my child) "I was so hoping you would come!" Her voice sounded just a bit stronger than the last time Nancy had visited or was she imagining it?

"Come here and talk to me," Grandma invited. Nancy pulled a small bench to the bedside and began her best recounting of neighborhood news. Grandma listened nodding and asking a question now and then. Finally, she placed a finger on the Bible resting in Nancy's lap.

"Read me something from that good Book."

Nancy opened to Psalm 121 and began. By the time she finished, Grandma's lids were drooping.

"Thank you, my child," she murmured.

Nancy bent to kiss this dear lady she'd grown to love so much.

"I love you," she whispered.

Grandma smiled and Nancy rose to leave. Laura's eyes met hers as she turned. They stepped toward the door and into the patio together.

"How has she seemed these last days?" Nancy questioned. "Any improvement? Is she eating? Taking her pills?"

"She is just contented to lie there by the fire. I urge her to come to the table and eat a bit with us. 'No, Hijita,' she answers. 'Just bring me a little if it's no trouble, when you have time.' I try to make some of her favorites. She eats a few bites and then says she's had enough. I give her a pill. She puts it in her mouth but later I find it under her pillow."

Nancy had to smile despite the seriousness of the situation.

"That rascal! Maybe if I run into San Diego for some of the puddings she likes so well... We can crush the pill in pudding. Maybe that will work."

"I hope so!" Laura sighed. "If there is a good papaya, could you bring me one? She loves papaya."

"Anything else you can think of that might spark her appetite?"

"Not right now."

"I'll look around."

"Thank you! Thank you, Nancy! I'll give you the pesos when you get back."

139

"No need, Laura. Let me just do this for Grandma. I want her to get better. We all love her so."

Laura nodded with another, "Thank you," tears near the surface.

Nancy continued daily visits to Grandma's bedside. The pills crushed in pudding seemed to be working. At least she was getting most of her medication. Nancy tried to take other tempting things that might tantalize Grandma's taste buds. She had brought an avocado along with the pudding and the papaya from town.

"She's eating a little better," Laura whispered on Nancy's next visit. "She asked for more papaya this morning and the avocado was a hit."

They clung to these fragile signs of improvement but deep inside they both knew they were not winning the battle.

Most afternoons Nancy would find Grandma sound asleep. She'd visit a while with Laura, hoping Grandma would waken. But, at last she'd have to give up and leave her gift on the table for later. The few times she did find Grandma responding, she took advantage of it for a short Bible reading and a prayer.

One such afternoon, Nancy leaned close to Grandma's ear. She'd pleaded earnestly in her prayer times for this opportunity.

"Grandma, are you very close to Jesus these days?" she questioned.

Grandma's eyes opened wide. She hadn't expressed such alertness in some time.

"Of course, Mi Hijita," she beamed. "He is right here with me. Don't you remember? You, yourself told me about Him and how He loves us so much. Remember? And I asked Him to forgive all the nasty things I have done. He did, Nancy, He did! And He is with me all the time!"

Grandma smiled and patted Nancy's hand. "Thank you, Mi Hijita, thank you!"

She grew quiet, the burst of energy depleted. Her eyelids drooped and she dozed, the smile still in place.

Spring was passing into summer as Grandma slowly deteriorated. Laura was stalwartly maintaining a brave front for Otoniel. The thought of losing his mother seemed unbearable to this rugged village farmer. His shoulders drooped; his eyes were sunken from lack of sleep. Nancy tried to spend as many nightly hours as possible watching over Grandma so the couple could get some rest.

This evening Grandma's going seemed eminent. Laura and Otoniel were exhausted. Nancy promised to call them at any indication. As the fragile lady's breathing grew more and more shallow, she stepped to the bedroom curtain and whispered. Otoniel sprang from bed, great heaving sobs racking his body. He fell to his knees beside his mother's cot. Laura followed placing her small warm hands around her husband's shoulders, her tears dampening his hair.

Grandma opened weary eyes to gaze at this her youngest son.

"Don't cry, Hijito. I'm going with Jesus. Be happy for me."

She was gone.

Nancy spent the night. She made coffee which Otoniel accepted sipping at it dejectedly. She urged Laura to eat a bit of the abandoned leftovers from supper. Toward morning she listened to their desires for the funeral. They would talk more with Enrique. In the villages, interment needed to be done without delay.

Otoniel rose. "I'll get the boards," he whispered. Jaime, having heard the news arrived to help make the coffin, insisting on doing most of the work.

Enrique and other neighbors were soon at the

door to make arrangements for digging the new grave. Laura brought a much treasured quilt to line Grandma's final resting place. Ofelia came with little Nathanael to help prepare Grandma for her funeral service.

Nancy offered to take Laura's three for breakfast. Over the meal she reassured the children of their grandmother's arrival in that most beautiful place called heaven.

"Jesus was waiting for her there. She isn't sick anymore and she is so very happy," Nancy concluded.

"We are sad, aren't we, Miss Nancy?" Josefina whispered. "But I'm very glad that Grandma is happy. Aren't you, Jose Luis?" Her brother nodded. "I am, too," Clarisa added solemnly.

Breakfast over, Myra and Nancy began the task of readying the church. The children helped by bringing armfuls of blossoms to be placed around the casket.

It had been decided to turn the church benches around facing out with the casket occupying the area in front of the open double doors. Relatives and close friends could fill the church itself. Overflow crowd, which there surely would be, could use the grassy space in front of the building.

The message had gone out by radio to San Diego and nearby villages. Sonya and Marco would have heard along with many others. These mourners would be trickling in. Food for the more distant visitors needed to be prepared. Myra and Nancy began this, another need, awaiting their attention.

Little groups of villagers could be seen arriving now on foot. Before long, Volkswagens and pickups from farther away began to be parked in every conceivable place along the village streets.

Miguel and his mother arrived from La Mesa to express their heartfelt regrets.

"If there's anything I can do, Otoniel," Miguel offered, "any late planting or other job I could help with… let me know."

Otoniel knew that he meant it and squeezed his neighbor's hand with a murmured, "Gracias".

The hour of service had arrived. The small church was filled. The crowd outside hushed as Enrique rose from his place on the church steps. Accompanying with his guitar, he led the crowd in two well-known hymns. Nancy's Bible story group sang "Jesus Loves Me". Then, Enrique read from Psalm 121, Grandma's favorite scripture passage. He spoke of the love and respect all of them had for this special lady, concluding with John 14:1-6. He told his audience that their neighbor and friend was now in the presence of this Jesus who is "the Way, the Truth and the Life". Going on, Enrique explained that she had invited this loving Lord into her life as Savior.

"And remember friends," he continued, "God sent His Son for each of us to receive as Savior and Lord of our lives. We, then, will join Grandma Victoria in the glories of heaven where, I'm very sure, she is clapping her hands and rejoicing today. If you would like, you may pray this prayer with me."

He proceeded to lead the gathered villagers in a prayer of repentance and acceptance of Jesus.

Pallbearers rose to escort the casket to the nearby burial grounds. At the graveside, mourners chose a flower from a well-filled basket. They filed by the coffin leaving their blossoms on top of the rustic box.

Words of commitment were repeated. And Grandma Victoria was placed in the hands of her loving Heavenly Father as the casket was lowered.

Chapter 16
"The Plans I Have For You"

Nancy closed her door behind her and began the usual trek for milk to Dona Chela's goat ranch. Huerfanita's appetite was ever increasing.

She spotted Otoniel striding toward her down the opposite side of the street. What a relief it was that now he didn't look away or quickly turn down a side street to avoid her.

"Good morning, Miss Nancy."

Crossing over, he met her with a smile and a handshake.

"How are you, Otoniel?"

"Much better now. I'm learning to accept this as God's best plan for my mother. He's giving me peace. Laura and I have wanted to thank you for

146

all you did at the funeral time. You and Myra were there for us at every turn. Thank you so much!"

"We have a question for you, Miss Nancy," he went on. "You know we've been trying to go God's way now. But it's all new to us. We have so many questions. Do you think you might have time for us, maybe once a week, to meet and go over some of these issues? We really do want to learn His ways."

"Of course, Otoniel. I'd be ever so happy to share what I've learned and experienced. I don't know all the answers, but we can search His Word together and get His guidance. When would be a good time?"

They agreed on day and time. Otoniel went on his way while Nancy continued her errand. Her heart lifted in joyful thanksgiving to the Lord who had accomplished the wondrous change in this man. She'd have good news for Myra. How often they had prayed together for Laura and Otoniel.

A timid knock called Nancy to her door shortly after lunch. The diminutive teen looked up shyly. Nancy knew Ana was a member of Enrique's youth group. She hadn't had a lot of opportunity to get well acquainted with the young girl.

"Miss Nancy, do you know I'm going to be fifteen years old in just five weeks?" the girl began.

"Oh Ana!" Nancy responded. "That's exciting!"

"Yes, Miss Nancy! I will be having my quinceanera soon." She hesitated. "Well, I was wondering if you would like to be one of my attendants."

"Why, yes, I would be delighted."

"Oh, thank you, Miss Nancy! The problem is, I don't know which to ask you to be."

Nancy waited puzzled.

Ana went on, "Since you are our missionary, I'd like you to be my attendant of the Bible. But on the other hand, there is no one else with a pretty little car like yours."

Another hesitation.

"So, could you be the attendant of the car? You see, with the big skirt of my quinceanera dress and in high heels, it would be difficult to walk all the way from the church to the hall."

"Is there a rule that says I can't be both?" Nancy queried smiling.

Ana giggled. "No, I guess not."

"Then I will be both. How is that?"

"Thank you! Thank you!" Nancy was engulfed

in a joyous hug.

As Ana went happily on her way, Nancy spied Myra busy in her patio next door.

"Myra," she called. "Is there a place where I can find a pretty white Bible and have Ana's name engraved on it?"

"She asked you to be her attendant of the Bible, didn't she?" Myra smiled.

"Yes, and I will also be her attendant of the car."

"Well, you are really getting involved in your first quinceanera in Puesta del Sol."

"And I'm delighted! Now I have a car, but where can I acquire a proper Bible?"

"I think Bibles are easier to come by than cars. But let's see… There is a bookstore in San Diego. I don't know if they carry the kind of Bible you would need. But, you know, we talked of your taking a trip to visit your family soon. You want to talk over the matter of your staying on here. While you're there, I imagine, you'll be able to find just the Bible you need."

Myra had a roll and coffee waiting as Nancy stepped into her kitchen in mid-afternoon. There was much to talk about and to take to the Lord in prayer.

First, of course, the news of Otoniel's request for some guidance in his and Laura's new life with God. Myra became a little teary-eyed as she thanked the Lord for this answer to their many prayers. They went on to the difficult subject neither wanted to face. Nancy's year in Puesta del Sol was coming to a close.

"You've called your mission, Nancy?"

"Yes. They tell me they have no one to replace me. Do you think that is the answer?"

"How I hope so! I'm trying so hard not to influence you. But…" she dropped her head to conceal her emotion. "I don't know how we can go on without you," she sighed. "Not even a replacement would be the same. It just wouldn't, Nancy."

Tears stung Nancy's eyes. Her voice was too choked to respond. She grasped Myra's hands and they shed their tears together.

Nancy wiped her eyes. "I'm praying so hard for a resolution. I know God isn't all confused like I am."

Myra had to smile. "God confused? No, I've never heard of that happening. You do need to talk this over with your family. Why don't you come for supper? Enrique can help us decide on a time for you to be away a little while."

Nancy brightened. "Thank you for being so understanding, Myra. I can't bear the thought of leaving Puesta del Sol and all of you dearest of people. It will help so much to talk this over face to face and be able to see the family's reaction. I'm sure God is preparing them if this is His plan."

She spent a long time talking the whole situation over again with the Lord that evening.

"How can I leave Myra, my prayer partner? How can I shorten the study time with Laura and Otoniel? They're just beginning their walk with You. Can I give up these Bible hour children? But I don't want to neglect my family if they need me. Show me your way, Heavenly Father!"

Difficult days followed. An arm went around her at church. She looked down into Dona Antonia's big brown eyes. How much fun they'd had together working on the Christmas play.

"You're not leaving us, are you, Miss Nancy?"

The children at Bible story time lingered at the door instead of the usual rush outside to play. Slowly they moved back in her direction.

"Miss Nancy," one of them began. "If we promise to be ever and ever so good in every Bible story time, you won't go away will you?"

"What are you children talking about?"

"Our mamas say you might have to go away and not come back. That isn't true, is it?"

Nancy sat down and drew these youngsters to her side.

"Children, you know how much Jesus loves you, don't you? Do you think He would want anything to happen that would be very sad for you and for me? I'm asking Him every night when I pray to give us His perfect answer. Can you wait just a few days 'til we know His plan for sure? His plan is a good plan for everyone, isn't it? Do you agree?"

"Yes! Yes! Because He loves us, He will give us His good plan!"

She drew the whole crowd of young ones into her arms for a big hug.

"And I love you, too, very much!"

It was a relief to turn the blue VW homeward on Tuesday morning. Several hours later she was heading her car up the familiar lane leading to the Jefferson's yard.

Mom was racing out the kitchen door to meet her.

"Welcome home, 'Mi Hijita'." Her eyes sparkled with mischief.

"So, all my family is now speaking Spanish," Nancy laughed.

"Well, I did learn that much from your phone calls. How many times you said someone had called you 'Mi Hijita' and how it warms your heart."

Mom's arm was around Nancy's waist.

"Come inside for some iced tea."

Sipping the welcome tea, Nancy studied her mother.

"How are you doing, Mom? Is there an awful lot of work these days?"

"Nancy, we have been so blessed! That Dan is a jewel! His hours at work have been changed some. He's doing more driving and delivery. He has a little more freedom. And what does he do but show up here to give us a hand with the yard and the farm tasks!"

"And Dad?"

He's doing well. Joey is growing into a real young farmer. He is a big help to your father. I know you've come home to talk over your big decision for next year. I have concerns about you, Dear, which I'm praying over much. Why don't we make time to talk this out together in the morning after breakfast?"

"Thank you, Mom. I'll so appreciate that."

It was a super farm breakfast they all enjoyed in the sunny kitchen.

"How about adjourning to the living room?" Dad suggested as they finished the last biscuits. "I like the softer chairs," he grinned.

"We miss you much, Nancy," he began. "But, as Mom has told you, it seems God has just made some special arrangements for help for us. Dan often has a delivery this way at the end of the day. He drops in here and checks on any yard and garden jobs that need doing. That relieves Mom. We invite him for supper and then he takes on a big share of evening chores. It's gotten to be a regular thing. Among the three of us," nodding at Joey, "it's quick work."

"I think your mother has some concerns she wants to mention."

"My biggest worry, Dear," Mom started, "is if you should get sick or hurt. Are there dangerous snakes, poisonous insects, mosquitoes that carry diseases? Where would you go and to whom for medical help?"

"Legitimate concerns," Dad agreed. "Can you put your mother at ease about such things and explain to us your situation and the needs at your village?"

"Mom, I have yet to see a snake there, not that there aren't any, but they don't seem to come into the village. As to the 'creepy crawlies' I did have that horrid tarantula in my patio but Enrique assures me they don't attack. The danger would be backing one into a corner. Believe me, I've stopped leaving my muddy boots outside the door. I'd not like to push my feet in beside one. I do use repellent for mosquitoes. Does that help you to feel better?"

"Where would you go if you got very sick?"

"There is a hospital in San Diego. Our Doctor Canales there has everyone's respect and confidence. I also am well stocked with antibiotics and other remedies at the house, you know."

"All that is comforting, Nancy," Mom agreed. "Go on, please. What are you feeling God wants in this?"

"Of course, last fall I understood I was only filling in for a year. I've called the Mission more than once, hoping someone was there to take my place. They just don't have anyone to send! I've prayed and prayed! I can't feel right about leaving Puesta del Sol without help. How often someone says, 'What if you hadn't been here?' and I agree. I don't know what would have happened to Clarisa, or worse, to Tomasito. But I did have to have your input in this decision.

"Mom?" Dad Jefferson questioned.

"What you've said, Nancy, has quieted much of my concerns. I shouldn't have said 'worries'. God doesn't want us to do that. I realize your need to continue there and I agree."

"Couldn't you come to visit with Dan at my break time to spend a couple of days? You could get acquainted with the village, see my little home, meet Myra, Laura and the others. I think that would help with any lingering qualms you have."

Mom turned to Dad. He was nodding.

"Do that, Mother," he encouraged.

"Daddy, Joey, you haven't voiced your opinions."

Joey had been unusually quiet but now he burst out.

"We miss you somethin' fierce, Nance. But you better do what God says. That's the only way! Besides," he went on, "if you stay I can visit and go to that fabulous Independence Day celebration with you. I'm sure our history teacher wouldn't want me to miss such a historical event. He might even give me an A+."

"Typical Joey," Nancy smiled. "You are the best little brother anyone ever had! And, yes, you should attend Mexico's Independence Day with me.

She looked at Dad.

"I believe this is of God," he agreed. "See how He has fitted everyone's needs into a perfect pattern. God's plans are always suited to everyone's needs. Isn't that amazing?"

Relief flooded Nancy's heart. This was her Heavenly Father's marvelous answer.

"Thank you, dear family! People are turning to God in Puesta del Sol: Don Tomas and his family, for example. It's not just me involved. God sees your willingness for me to be there. We're doing this together."

"Amen!" Dad spoke for everyone.

Chapter 17
The Quinceanera

All of Puesta del Sol seemed to be in a flurry preparing for Ana's quinceanera. Village ladies joined Ana's mother in busily shaping colored paper into attractive table decorations. Others were scrubbing the village hall to a perfect shine. The Mariachi band was coming together. Miguel and his cousin would participate with their violins. A friend of the family in San Diego agreed to be there with his trumpet. Enrique promised to join with his guitar.

Trip after trip to San Diego was necessary to acquire all the finery needed. Nancy took Ana on a search for violet and rose-colored flowers to decorate the hall. They needed to bring rolls of white paper suitable for table cloths as well.

Ana seemed to lose her shyness on the excursion and chattered giddily all the way.

"Do you know who is going to be my escort, Miss Nancy?"

"Why, no, Ana. Who did you choose?"

Ana blushed a little. "Javier agreed to escort me. Isn't that nice? He is very tall and handsome, as well as polite and proper. I like him," she giggled.

"Yes, he surely is a special boy. He was one of those who played soccer when Joey was here. He taught Joey Spanish words and tried to make him feel like one of the team."

"If Joey would be here, I would choose him for my escort," Ana announced.

"He would be honored and delighted, Ana. But it is probably best that you have chosen one of the village young people to take part. They might feel left out."

"Yes, I guess that is best," Ana agreed. "I wouldn't want them to feel that way."

After quite a search, the trip finally yielded the very shades of flowers Ana had in mind. She chose small silver baskets to hold her bouquets. They would adorn the tables along with the ornaments made by her mother and friends.

They twisted and turned, pushed and pried in the attempt to accommodate the large rolls of white paper in the reduced space behind the car's front seats. The problem was solved at last by sliding the seats forward enough to wedge the rolls in.

"Oh!" Ana exclaimed breathless and relieved. "I thought we were going to have to leave them here!"

"But we made it!" Nancy sighed. "Shall we go have some ice cream to cool off and relax?"

"Oh, Miss Nancy, that would be lovely! But I have spent all my money."

"Well, I think I have enough for ice cream," Nancy winked.

And they went merrily on their way for a fine conclusion to the day's efforts.

Sandwiched between the excitement and demands of the preparations for the quinceanera, Nancy met for study with Otoniel and Laura. She was thrilled and amazed by the extent and depth of their searching questions. After one particularly productive session, Otoniel couldn't contain himself.

"Miss Nancy," he exclaimed, "I have to share this with other men! Most of us villagers, myself included, have thought being Christian was a boring, rule-keeping existence that suffocates all of life's enjoyments. It is not that! It's challenge! It's excitement! It's a whole new outlook! Sure, there are regrets, even grief, but Jesus gives peace because He has forgiven and renewed us. Miss Nancy, can I bring another couple to our study if they will come?"

"Of course, Otoniel! That would be excellent."

The following week Jaime and Ofelia arrived at study time.

"May we join you?" Ofelia smiled.

"Welcome to both of you!" Nancy responded. "We're so happy to have you."

With Otoniel's contagious enthusiasm catching on among his neighbors, the study group began to grow.

Nancy would not soon forget the children's first Bible hour after her return from home. Little Felix marched up to her. Planting his feet solidly apart he declared, "You aren't going away, are you, Miss Nancy!"

"No, Felix, I am not!" she replied.

He snapped his tiny fingers above his head.

"I knew it! Because Jesus loves us!"

Ana tapped at Nancy's door.

"Tomorrow is the day!" she announced bubbling over with excitement and anticipation. "Is my 'chariot' ready?"

"It is all washed and polished, Ana, just waiting for the honored passenger to step inside."

"Could I practice getting in? Of course, I will have my big skirt to manage tomorrow. But maybe we can just see how that will be possible."

"Yes, Ana, let's give it a try. Maybe if I slide the driver's seat forward as far as it will go that will help."

"I hope you don't have to push me in like the rolls of tablecloth paper," Ana laughed.

"I don't believe you're as big as they," Nancy reassured her, smiling.

Their plan seemed workable. Once Ana was comfortably seated in the back, Nancy would have to slide the front seat in place again in order to drive… a little awkward but something they could manage.

The celebration was to begin at the church at 11:00 am. Nancy parked her car at Ana's home with plenty of extra minutes for Ana to adjust herself and her gorgeous gown in her "chariot".

Javier met them on the front lawn of the church regally attired in his fine rented tuxedo. With his help, Ana was able to make a graceful exit from Nancy's vehicle.

He gazed at her in all the beauty of her rose-colored gown, billowing skirt and modest neckline covered with tiny pearls and sequins. Her hair was swept back hanging in ringlets from a flowered hair piece. Tiny curls framed her face.

"You look beautiful," he whispered.

"Thank you. And you, very elegant," she returned.

As they stepped into the church aisle all heads turned. Whispered approval and admiration ceased as Enrique rose and stood at the pulpit.

Javier guided Ana expertly to her decorated "throne" at the front and then seated himself.

First, Enrique was to proceed with a few affirmations to which Ana should declare her assent.

Very formally he addressed the radiant teen seated before him.

"Ana Lopez Sandoval, do you believe in God, the Father, Creator and Sustainer of His entire universe and of your very life?"

"I do!" she promptly answered.

"Ana Lopez Sandoval do you acknowledge Jesus Christ, God's only Son as your Lord and Savior?"

"Yes Sir, I do!"

"Ana Lopez Sandoval, do you at this time purposefully yield your life and your future into God's hands with perfect trust in his love and unerring provision throughout the days He grants you on this earth?"

An earnest "I do."

Enrique then began a brief informal message of caring admonitions for Ana. He reassured her of the love and support of the whole church congregation to which there were several "amens" from the gathered crowd. He commended her for her joyous participation in all that was asked of her. Whether at church or youth group, never was there a "no" or an "I can't" from Ana.

Enrique finished with a heartfelt prayer for this young lady whom they all had known and loved from childhood. The more serious part of the service concluded, the celebration took on a lighter tone as Enrique announced, "Will the attendant of the Bible please come forward."

Ana stood as Nancy reached her side and placed the beautiful white Bible in her hands. There was spontaneous clapping.

"Thank you! Thank you, Miss Nancy," Ana whispered. "I never thought I would have such a lovely, lovely Bible."

"The attendant of the ring, please," Enrique continued.

Ana's sister, Elsa, stepped forward. Opening the small case, she slipped a dainty ring on Ana's finger. She lingered a moment to give Ana a happy hug.

Ana's Grandmother, Elia, needed a little assistance when she was called upon but she proudly fastened the necklace, a prized family heirloom, about her granddaughter's throat and bent to place a kiss on the girl's cheek.

Ana's best friend, Reyna, was given the honor of fitting the matching bracelet on Ana's wrist.

"And now our final attendant," Enrique smiled, "the attendant of Ana's last doll."

Felisa, representing the whole youth group, waltzed merrily down the aisle. She carried a cuddly baby doll to place in Ana's arms.

When the chuckling subsided, Enrique spoke again.

"We are all now cordially invited to the village hall where we will continue this celebration."

Ana and Javier waited until all the guests were well on their way down the village street. Nancy, with Javier's help, assisted Ana into the car again. He took his place beside Nancy in the front seat.

As Ana and Javier stood at the hall door, the Mariachis struck up a spritely Mexican tune. There was toe tapping and hand clapping. As the music ended a jolly "Ole!" was heard from a listener across the hall.

The celebrated couple found their lavishly decorated seats at the head table. They faced the guests accommodated at two long arrangements which stretched the length of the hall.

Cooks bustled from the kitchen carrying large bowls of their favorite culinary successes. These were set at intervals along the table since food was to be served and passed family style.

When, at last, the elaborate meal was over the crowd settled back for an afternoon of more music, gift opening and games. A huge box sat beside Ana's chair causing interest and curiosity. At the insistence of everyone, she began the task of tearing away paper and prying back the stiff cover.

"Oh!" she exclaimed at the sight of another sealed container inside. Javier came to her aid, helping to lift out the second box and moving aside the clutter. To Ana's surprise, the second box only revealed a third. A fourth and fifth box followed. There was laughter. Finally, she reached the small beautifully wrapped box number six. She tore aside paper to reveal a most welcome devotional book.

"There's something inside," Javier whispered. Ana drew out an envelope and its contents. A small note was wrapped around several bills. It read, "Accept this, Ana, to pay for piano lessons when you return to school in San Diego this fall. Our love, Enrique and Myra."

Ana wiped away tears. How she had longed to study piano, but there had never been enough money for lessons.

"With all my heart, I thank you! And when Puesta del Sol Church has a piano, I will be the pianist. Mr. Enrique and I will play together!"

The Mariachis' lively music filled the hall again. The young people and some adults played games. Too soon it was time for the late afternoon refreshments.

At last each guest had departed. The faithful blue "chariot" was called upon to carry Ana to her own doorstep. She thanked Javier graciously for being such a fine and attentive escort.

"Oh, Miss Nancy," she went on. "Wasn't it wonderful! I wish it wasn't over but I am s-o-o-o tired!"

"It was the most beautiful party I have ever attended," Nancy agreed. "It was precious! Now you must rest and dream of your glorious day. Until tomorrow."

Chapter 18
I Understand, Mi Hijita

Nancy had overslept. After bidding Ana goodbye yesterday afternoon, she had returned to help tidy the hall. Then, she had dropped quite exhausted on her own sofa bench at home. But what an unbelievably successful God-honoring day it had been.

"I'll just relax a few minutes here," she sighed.

Abruptly Nancy sat erect.

"What day is this? Mom and Dan will be here tomorrow! I'd better get to bed so I can function in the morning."

Friday afternoon Nancy watched expectantly for the pickup Dan would be driving. She'd just given a final pat to the bed pillow where

Mom would sleep when a horn sounded outside.

"They're here!" she announced to Huerfanita. The kitten followed her to the door. Dan was helping Mom Jefferson step down from the pickup.

Nancy dashed to meet them.

Mom was bubbling with excitement. "Nancy!" she exclaimed. "This is a beautiful little village—so many flowers in front of homes! People even waved to us as we drove in!"

"They knew you were coming and are anxious to meet you. Come inside! See my little home. Tomorrow we'll do some visiting."

"I'll just grab these suitcases and the box of goodies from the truck bed," Dan offered.

Mom had spotted Huerfanita.

"Oh, here is your little kitty. How beautiful!" She gave Huerfanita a love pat.

"Where did you have lunch?" Nancy questioned as they settled around her table for coffee and a cookie.

"We ate before crossing the border," Dan replied. "So, it's been awhile. I could really use another one of those good cookies."

She passed him the plate.

It wasn't long before a hesitant tapping was heard at the door. Myra cracked it open and peered inside.

"I just couldn't wait," she half apologized, "to meet your mama and besides I want to know what you prefer for supper. You're eating with us, you know."

Nancy's mother had risen from her chair with arms outstretched.

"Myra! It's such a joy to meet you!" Nancy translated.

"Oh!" Mom Jefferson clapped her fingers to her mouth. "I forgot! I wish I could speak Spanish so we could talk and talk. Tell her, please, Nancy how happy I am for all she means to you and how she put my heart at rest when you first came here."

There was a little interchange of conversation and then Myra took a step toward the door.

"I didn't mean to barge in so soon on your arrival. Just tell me what you'd like for supper and I'll start the preparations. Enrique brought me chicken from San Diego. Would you enjoy chicken and rice?"

"Oh, yes, Myra. I know everyone would like that."

Nancy explained to the guests who both heartily agreed.

"Flan for dessert?"

"Yes! Yes! Wonderful, Myra!"

"Then, I'm off to start the meal. See you soon."

The lively conversation over supper kept Nancy on her toes. First it was Spanish to English and then English to Spanish. She was a bit breathless when it came time to say, "Good night".

Dan, of course, would spend the night in the same guest room offered to him on his former visit.

Mom and Nancy were soon comfortably situated, both ready to rest after a most exciting day.

Saturday had to be devoted to visiting all those Nancy wanted Mom Jefferson to meet.

Dan accompanied them up to Laura's patio primarily to see again the three children he had enjoyed so much before.

Having been told that the "pretty" American man was coming, Clarisa was the first to run laughingly in his direction. He caught her and swung her into his arms. He offered his free hand to Josefina. Jose Luis followed at his side as Laura called them into the house to meet Miss Nancy's mama.

"Is our Miss Nancy your little girl?" Josefina wanted to know.

"That's right," Mom responded.

Typical of Jose Luis, his words were few. After gazing into Mom's face a few moments, he murmured, "We like Miss Nancy."

Adult conversation began to tire the children. Dan addressed Nancy. "Ask them if they want to play tag."

"Yes! Yes!" They followed Dan to the patio for a few minutes of darting and dodging as Dan pretended he couldn't catch them. The ladies appeared at the door.

"We need to go on, Laura. Thank you for the cool drinks."

Mom laid a hand on Nancy's arm. "Please tell Laura how I am enjoying the doilies she sent at Christmas."

Laura smiled and hugged this lady she was so happy to have just now met. Moments later the visitors sat in Ofelia's kitchen. Mom reached out her arms to little Nathanael and he extended his chubby hands to her.

"May I hold him?" she asked.

Ofelia smiled and nodded.

The little guy was soon patting this nice lady's soft hair. Expertly he entwined his little fingers into strands of hair and began to pull.

Ofelia jumped to the rescue. Then she began to recount the story of Nathanael's name for Mrs. Jefferson as Nancy translated.

Mom Jefferson could scarcely contain the pride she sensed at the beautiful tribute to her daughter.

As they walked down the hill, Mom said softly, "I am thankful you were here to safeguard the birth of that baby. I am so thankful."

Reaching the street below, they met Enrique with his team of oxen. He waved at Dan.

"Come help me."

Dan glanced at Nancy.

"He'd like you to go with him. Go ahead. We just have one more visit to make."

"OK, see you then."

The men turned toward Enrique's maturing corn field.

"You want to drive my oxen?"

Dan understood a couple of the man's words. As Enrique put the lines in his hands, he realized that he was invited to manage this team of huge animals. Enrique called directions and the oxen moved ahead. The lines tightened. Dan held on. Back and forth they plodded along the rows of corn as Enrique cut and piled the green stalks into the cart. The cows would relish this fodder while they were being milked.

Enrique again got a message across to Dan. Pointing to him, he made the milking motion. Dan laughed and nodded.

What fun they had! Enrique let the cows into the corral. They each sat on an upturned bucket and made the milk sing in the pails they held between their knees.

The ladies had walked several blocks.

"I want you to meet Ana, Mom, the girl that had her quinceanera this past week. Maybe she will model her gorgeous dress for you."

Ana met them at the door of her home. "Miss Nancy! And this is your mother! I'm sorry Mama isn't here. She and my sisters went to help Grandma this afternoon. I'm getting the beans cooked while they are gone. Come in!"

"I've been telling my mother about your quinceanera, Ana, especially about the beautiful dress we had to tuck into my car," Nancy smiled.

"Would you like to see my dress, Mrs. Jefferson?" Ana asked.

"Indeed, I would!" Mom responded.

"If Miss Nancy will help me, I'll put it on." After a few minutes the two emerged from the

Lopez girls' bedroom. Ana twirled and curtsied.

"What a gorgeous gown! You must have had such a lovely celebration," Mom concluded.

"I have to tell you a most wonderful part, Mama Jefferson. I was given a gift to pay for piano lessons! Our church doesn't have a piano yet, but when it does I will help Mr. Enrique play the hymns and we will have beautiful music."

Mrs. Jefferson looked at her daughter. "Nancy, remember that keyboard we have upstairs? We don't use it now. Wouldn't that work for them here until they can get a piano?"

"Mom! That's a great idea! Ana could practice on it when she is home weekends."

She turned to explain to Ana. The girl jumped for joy. She hugged "Mama" Jefferson and then she hugged Nancy.

"Oh, I've never been so happy," she cried.

"Then I'll bring it back," Nancy assured her, "after this fall break I'm taking."

They left an ecstatic little girl as they bid her goodbye.

The two ladies turned toward Nancy's home. Once inside they sank down on the sofa bench together.

"That was a long walk, Mom. Are you OK?"

"Perfectly OK. I enjoyed it all so much. Isn't that Ana a sweetie!"

"I'm so glad you thought of the keyboard, Mom. I'm sure we can get it across the border for her. She will be overjoyed."

"You'll meet more of the villagers at church tomorrow," Nancy went on.

"Wonderful! I am seeing how much you are needed here, Nancy. Will the family of the little boy who nearly drowned be there?"

"They will. There just wasn't time or energy left to visit them this afternoon, but you'll meet the whole family tomorrow."

Dan joined them.

"Guess what I did," he chortled. "I drove oxen and I milked cows! Enrique meant it when he said, 'come help me.' It was a lot of fun. Just think what I can tell the fellows at the shop."

Everyone, of course, wanted to greet and chat with Nancy's mother on Sunday morning. How often one and another repeated the phrase: "I don't know how we could get along without her."

Don Tomas pressed her hand and with great emotion thanked her for the daughter who had saved his son.

"Come here, Tomasito. I want you to shake hands with Miss Nancy's mama."

"Miss Nancy made me breathe," the bright-eyed child declared.

Otoniel stopped Nancy on her way out of church.

"I've been thinking since you'll be gone a couple of weeks, why don't I give one of those studies we had before the others joined us? I have my notes."

"Otoniel that solves my problem! I hated to let the study go for these two times."

"All right then I'll do it; and if you could lend that Bible story book you sometimes read to the children, Laura says she can read to them on Mondays."

"Oh, thank you, Otoniel. That does relieve me so much."

On Sunday afternoon, everyone opted for some rest from the wondrous but taxing schedule of the previous day. In late afternoon, they roused themselves, snacked a bit and walked outside.

"Dan, look! There's going to be a gorgeous sunset. Shall we walk up to the other side of the village so as not to miss any of it? Mom, do you want to come along?"

178

"Thank you, Dear, but I'll just sit here in the patio and enjoy it."

"Nancy, I've been thinking," Dan began as they stepped into the street. "Could a fellow like me be of some use in the kind of work you are doing?"

"Yes, Dan. A 'fellow like you' could be a lot of use. These farmers need help. Drip irrigation could save their crops at times. You could teach them that. You could repair their tools, perhaps bring in some new implements. Remember the saying 'what you do speaks louder than what you say.'"

"And you know I am studying Spanish just in case the 'saying' might help on occasion," he interjected.

"Of course, it would. You would win their hearts. They would begin to question. 'Dan, why did you come to this primitive place when you could probably live in luxury on the other side of the border? Why are you doing this for us?

"Then comes the opportunity to tell them," Dan agreed, "of the wondrous love of Jesus which compels us to share His message of forgiveness and a changed life. God has been prodding me, Nancy. Right now, I want to help your folks. But a time is coming, I believe, when He wants me in ministry."

He stopped walking. She looked up at him.

"Maybe right here, Nancy. It would be quite special to work side by side with you." He looked away. Maybe he had said too much.

They stood now in the cactus patch from which they had viewed the sunset once before. His words echoed in her thoughts. Was Dan suggesting something deeper than their present friendship? Only God knew the answer to that. She would leave it with Him.

Slowly the glorious sunset was fading. Hand in hand they turned back toward the darkening village. Their hearts sang praises to the Divine Artist whose handiwork had just filled them with wonder. Joy overflowed at the assurance that God's message of love, pardon and peace was theirs to share with all dwellers beneath His tangerine skies.

The End

About the Author

Carol Wonch (Karelyn Kline) is a native of Michigan. She has spent most of her adult life ministering in Spanish-speaking areas including several years in the mountain villages of Mexico. She now resides in south Texas among her Hispanic friends and neighbors.

Got an idea for a book? Contact Curry Brothers Marketing and Publishing Group, LLC. We are not satisfied until your publishing dreams come true. We specialize in all genres of books, especially religion, leadership, family history, poetry, and children's literature. There is an African Proverb that confirms, *"When an elder dies, a library closes."* Be careful who tells your family history. Are their values your family's values? Our staff will navigate you through the entire publishing process, and take pride in going the extra mile by exceeding your publishing goals.

Improving the world one book at a time!

Curry Brothers Books, LLC
PO Box 247
Haymarket, VA 20168
(719) 466-7518 & (615) 347-9124
Visit us at www.currybrothersbooks.com